Reading Like a Serpent

Reading Like a Serpent

What the Scarlet A Is About

MARILYN CHANDLER MCENTYRE

for Heather and Logan —
Wise readers, indeed.
With love,
Marilyn

CASCADE *Books* · Eugene, Oregon

READING LIKE A SERPENT

What the Scarlet A Is About

Cascade Books
An Imprint of Wipf and Stock Publishers
199 W. 8th Ave., Suite 3
Eugene, OR 97401

www.wipfandstock.com

ISBN 13: 978-1-61097-554-4

Cataloging-in-Publication data:

McEntyre, Marilyn Chandler

    Reading like a serpent : what the scarlet a is about / Marilyn Chandler McEntyre.

    x + 134 p. ; 23 cm. Includes bibliographical references.

    ISBN 13: 978-1-61097-554-4

    1. Hawthorne, Nathaniel, 1804–1864. Scarlet letter. 2. Puritans in literature. 3. Women in literature. I. Title.

PS 1868 .M84 2012

Manufactured in the U.S.A.

For John,
who reads to me and with me,
with love and thanks for making sure I wrote this book.
Your imprint is on every page.
For Mary, Elizabeth, and Margaret,
who understand why I love Hester Prynne
and her little Pearl.
I give thanks for the little girls you were and the women you are.
and
in grateful memory of
Emory Elliott,
whose teaching of American literature
has long informed my own

"... be ye therefore wise as serpents and harmless as doves."

Matthew 10:16

Contents

Preface

THIS BOOK IS NOT primarily intended as a work of literary criticism or scholarship, though I have benefited from the long, rich discussion of *The Scarlet Letter* that critics and scholars have fostered. Rather it is a series of personal reflections on how Hawthorne's literary techniques serve purposes whose urgency we still have reason to recognize. I hope it will induce readers to reread his with renewed appreciation of the deep character of his ambivalences, annoyances, and longings, especially with respect to the continuing conversation about how to read the texts, both sacred and secular, that shape our self-understandings and our life together.

Since I quote so frequently from *The Scarlet Letter*, and have taken quoted passages from the free online version provided by the generously funded Gutenberg Project, I have chosen to omit page numbers when referring to that text. All quoted passages may be easily located by a word-search in the Gutenberg text.

Where I quote the Bible in these chapters it is always from the King James Version, as most in keeping with what Hawthorne's readers would have heard and read.

Part I

—✦—

A Prophet at Play

Who among those of us who attended American public schools does not remember our first encounter with Hester Prynne, the hapless heroine of *The Scarlet Letter*? Served up to sixteen-year-olds as standard fare, often sandwiched between Edgar Allan Poe (whose "The Pit and the Pendulum" was, let us admit, far more gripping stuff) and Emily Dickinson (all of whose poems, someone has pointed out, can be sung to "The Yellow Rose of Texas," which makes it hard to grasp their depth and cunning at first glance), this quaint and curious tale has, in fact, failed to delight generations of young readers. Not all, to be sure, but I find, because I always ask when we embark on our return visit to this little American classic in college courses, that many students recall *The Scarlet Letter* as stiff, boring, wordy, moralistic, lacking in plot, and generally incomprehensible. So when I tell them it is one of my two or three favorite books in the world and has withstood considerable comparison in my long reading life, their curiosity is piqued—either about the hidden merits of the book or about my taste and credibility. Some of them, no doubt, think I really ought to get a life.

It is my privilege thereupon to lead them once again, the reluctant, the skeptical, the compliant, and the happy, eager few, into the thickets of Hawthorne's antique syntax, to show them how to navigate the interpretive mazes he maps for his readers, and to witness the epiphanies that ensue. *The Scarlet Letter* is a book deeply occupied with reading and interpretation—most urgently with the ways we read Scripture, and consequently, history. The heart of its message is not about the sin of adultery (a word not mentioned once in the story) but rather about the sin of bad reading and the many sins that ensue from bad reading practices, especially when Scripture is read badly. Most egregious among these readerly sins are literalism, legalism, and misapplied allegorical or typological thinking.

The generation of readers Hawthorne addressed—educated New England folk weaned on sermons, and moralistic hornbooks—were also heirs to a Puritan legacy he himself found troubling, if not repugnant. Indeed, Hawthorne may be among those most responsible for giving the Puritans a bad name. A good many scholars of American Puritanism would assure us that those early settlers, for all the mistakes and cross-cultural offenses we might lay at their feet, were a complex, God-loving as well as God-fearing people, capable of beautiful music, lively poetry, and delight in the gifts of farm and family. But Hawthorne brooded on how his own bloodline led back to John Hathorne, the severest judge in the New England witch trials. He wrestled with the limitations of popular piety in churches he reluctantly attended.[1] His travels to Italy as an adult fed a fascination with Roman Catholicism that shows up in many of his stories, especially the last. In that novel, *The Marble Faun*, a young American girl repeatedly described as a child of the Puritans finds her way into the basilica of St. Peter's. Longing for release from her own anxieties about sin, she enters a confessional where a kindly priest, though he cannot give her absolution, comforts her, apparently, among other things, for the spiritual forfeitures of the Protestant Reformation, one of those being the relief of the sacrament of confession. In his home in Concord, Hawthorne hung a reproduction of Raphael's lovely Madonna. Two of his daughters became nuns, one an Anglican, the other a Roman Catholic. The latter—his little

---

1. Actually, Hawthorne criticizes the organized religion of both his own and the Puritan times, preferring the "narrow but earnest cushion-thumper" of Puritanical times to the "cold, lifeless, vaguely liberal clergyman" of his own. But he rejects both, indicating a general antipathy for clergymen, whose work, "for the most part," is "stupendous impertinence." Stewart, ed., *The American Notebooks*, 158, quoted in Austin, *College English*, 61.

Rose, later known to the world as Mother Alfonsa—has been beatified and is now a candidate for canonization.

Still, he himself did not convert, but lived in prolonged and uncomfortable reflection on the legacy of personal and collective "sin and sorrow" that held him captive to some extent and fueled an ambivalent interest in the terms of Protestant piety throughout his life. He shared with many socially conscious thinkers of his generation a fascination with the complexities of language, reading, and interpretation, and with how Scripture could be and was being read and misread. Along with Emerson, Thoreau, Melville, and others, he recognized the enormous social consequences of oversimplified, legalistic biblical literalism, and bent his own considerable intelligence to teaching readers to read more complexly, imaginatively, and audaciously.

His concern with reading also extended to the nature of historical narrative: how we receive, retell, and read the record of history.[2] He understood how much imagination, and how many shaping assumptions, are at work in any representation of history. In writing an historical novel, he raises, both implicitly in the narrative itself and explicitly in the introductory "Custom House" section, the vexing questions of what it means to tell the truth about the past, what are the legitimate uses of the past, and what is the relationship of history to mythmaking.

For Hawthorne, history is most importantly parable. In *The Scarlet Letter* he borrows from and plays with the conventions of history and parable, and also of legend, novel, romance, satire, and sermon. This generic ambiguity serves a number of purposes, the most important of which is to call our attention to interpretive frames: our conclusions about the story's meaning will vary considerably according to how we read it—and multiple valid interpretations are possible. Like Melville and others who took an interest in the beginnings of "higher criticism," a controversial academic approach to biblical texts, Hawthorne was disaffected by the New England church, convinced that the Bible was being both misread and misapplied by a lineage of literalists and Pharisees. He was disturbed by how certain strands of moralistic preaching and popular piety suppressed the ambiguities of Scripture and made the Bible an instrument of control.

---

2. See Gretchen Jordan, "Hawthorne's Bell," for a discussion of his philosophy of history. She claims that his tales proceed through generations of American history and are an attempt to fathom the process of history-making.

One of his evident purposes in *The Scarlet Letter* is to invite his readers to critical biblical reflection and, in that process, to teach them how to read more responsibly, more reflectively, more generously, and more wittily. To ask a Christian audience, and his would have been almost entirely that in 1850 New England, to reflect on the nature of language and text was, of course, necessarily to raise the issue of how to approach biblical language and the biblical text, those being the foundation of moral, spiritual, and even political instruction. The Bible was the book that provided the frame for the discursive world his readers inhabited. The story told in *The Scarlet Letter* is replete with echoes of gospel narratives: of the woman caught in adultery, of Pharisees' hypocrisy and institutional oppression, of wrestling with demons, of the Sermon on the Mount, of passion and crucifixion.

Hawthorne plays freely with the material in the Gospels and, in an elaborate web of allusion, links the ancient story of salvation to the story of the settlement of New England. This analogy was certainly not original: by the time he inherited it from the Puritan settlers the notion of New England as a new Eden, a new wilderness, or a new Jerusalem had already shaped public life and legitimated questionable legal presumptions about entitlement to land. In the spirit of that legacy of analogy then, though giving it his own ironic spin, he assigned the story of early New England its own mythic status and offered it as a prototype for understanding the tensions of his own generation. In doing so, he situates himself squarely in the tradition of forebears who had seen the settlement of New England as a "type" of exile that replayed the wandering of the Israelites, God's people, in the desert, or, alternatively, as a godly people called forth to inhabit the New World as a New Eden, whose purposes and theology were already mapped in the Old and New Testaments. But he turns that tradition to his own ironic, satirical, and deeply serious purposes, calling our attention to its dangers, among which perhaps the most egregious is the way a self-justifying agenda of exploration and settlement had legitimated insularity, greed, and self-righteousness. The redemptive message he offers in the midst of this jeremiad is that there is another way—of reading, of opening the heart to divine and human encounter, of living together in more equitable fellowship. The allegorical habits of mind that lingered in popular folklore and fiction (American Christians at the time grew up on Bunyan and Aesop) seemed to him to narrow the imagination and truncate the mysterious, and even fanciful, ways the mind might arrive at meaning. Those ways, he implies, might be far more trustworthy than was commonly believed.

As a parable, *The Scarlet Letter* holds up a mirror to North American descendants of the early English settlers, inviting them to question the terms on which settlement and governance were established, and particularly to consider the destruction, loss, and guilt that project had left in its wake. He aimed his sharpest satirical barbs at those who clung to the letter of the law and who, like their ancestors, imposed the weight of the law more heavily on those guilty of sexual crimes (easy to target and titillating to the public imagination) than on those who abused or self-servingly wielded the powers of church and state. (This tendency may sound familiar, gentle readers. I urge you to consider readily available contemporary analogies.)

Each of the four central characters in *The Scarlet Letter*—Hester Prynne, Arthur Dimmesdale, Roger Chillingworth, and Pearl—is rich with dimensionality and symbolic suggestion. Each manifests a permutation of a few central ideas: that every individual carries the mark of sin, that individuals in community are inextricably and subtly bound to each other in the body politic, as also in the body of Christ, and in something like what Whitman subsequently called the "body electric" or what Martin Luther King called the "beloved community"—a natural environment of shared energies, vulnerabilities, and purposes not always conscious. In their inextricable interdependence, the characters challenge entrenched notions of individualism, as well as challenging whatever criteria we bring to judgment of character. Their fates are so intertwined, they are virtually impossible to consider independently. And there's an emphatic point to this careful and conspicuous interweaving: no one can be judged alone, apart from the social context in which his or her sin or virtue takes shape. It turns out, in their world as in this one, that none is righteous, that all have sinned, and that the sins, not only of the fathers, but of mothers and neighbors, are visited upon all God's children. Adversaries are counterparts, bound as deeply together in their hatred as brothers in their love. And sinfulness is a contaminant we all breathe and inhabit.

So Hester, Arthur, Roger, and Pearl have won a permanent place in the American imagination—or at least in American school curricula. But arguably, the most interesting character in *The Scarlet Letter* is the narrator. This narrator has irritated and confused generations of readers (especially hapless adolescents who wish he'd just get on with the plot). He gives with one hand and takes with another. He offers judgments, reconsiders, then abdicates altogether with a "be that as it may," or a "so it was said," or a coy observation that it were improper, indelicate, or untimely to arrive at a conclusive assessment of the incidents just recounted. He revels in paradox, inference, and indeterminacy. He keeps tossing us readers the ball he's been juggling, sometimes addressing us directly, standing in liminal space and time with one foot outside the frame, at times privy to the most intimate thoughts and feelings of the characters, and at other times abjectly dependent upon hearsay and scraps of barely decipherable evidence, like an historian facing frustrating gaps in a partial and dubious record. We get what we get from him by means of a cunning indirection that forces us into more active, critical, and self-critical reading.

The whole introductory narrative, "The Custom House," serves to raise fascinating and troubling questions about the uses of the past and the nature of historical narrative. If, as he suggests, the texts and artifacts that connect us to the past acquire meaning only by means of subjective and uncertain attribution, in what sense are they reliable? The narrator of this putatively historical/autobiographical note (which, however, is also fiction) hews very close to the author's younger self—an employee in a Salem custom house where he finds an old artifact, a scarlet A embroidered in gold—in a trunk, and begins a course of research and speculation to satisfy his curiosity about its origin and meaning. One point made repeatedly there and in the subsequent story is that what we take to be true and meaningful always comes to us through filters of speculation and inference. This insistence on the ubiquity of interpretation is not simply an early postmodernist rejection of absolute truth, but rather a reminder that we see through a glass darkly. That reminder turns into a warning worthy of the most ardent jeremiads of the Puritan preachers: beware those who claim to know the truth, the whole truth, and nothing but the truth. Beware also, he would add, of the literalists and legalists who turn the letter to their own purposes and ignore the Spirit.

The narrator who emerges in the story proper falls into a lineage one critic has described as "fictional transfigurations of Jesus."[3] If we can in any sense call Melville's Billy Budd or Dostoevsky's Prince Mishkin or C. S. Lewis's Aslan or Tolkien's Gandalf "Christ figures"—as all of them have been called—we must surely extend that category to include the nameless speaker in this singular American classic. He speaks to us as Americans

3. Ziolkowski, *Fictional Transfigurations of Jesus*.

and heirs of a very troubled Christian, Protestant, Puritan spiritual legacy, inviting us to a new understanding of our own sordid history, to reconsideration of its premises and to repentance for the abuses and infidelities that have shaped our ends as a nation. Echoing and invoking the Gospels at every turn, this narrator turns our attention first to "our" ancestors and their shortcomings, and, through them, to ourselves, if we are among the heirs of the dominant and domineering culture they established in this "new world." As a tale of sin and sorrow, repentance, penitence, and the renewal of minds, it recasts the biblical story in which the speaker is the teacher (full of rabbinical wit and riddling) and the teller of parables, inviting his hearers to active discernment if they have ears to hear. Deeply preoccupied with the history of his people, this narrator turns that history to his own partially veiled purpose—a prophetic rehearsal of how history tends toward myth and legend, how we shape it to our immediate ends, and how self-serving those ends tend to be.

His strategies are many, and his aims complex. In the coming pages, I will explore this narrator's tendency, for instance, to elicit judgment by indirection, implication, obliquity, and allusiveness; to align his sympathies first with one character and then with another, destabilizing our efforts to assess situations from a single point of view; to beg large theological questions such as how God is present in "Nature" by assuming but not naming that presence, intelligence, and intentionality; to dislocate us in time and space by making his observations from multiple historical and spatial vantage points; to indulge in wordplay that repeatedly calls our attention to the inevitable slippage of language itself; and, in short, to play the fool, in the best Shakespearean sense.

In doing so, the narrator falls into a long lineage of tricksters, teachers, and holy men who bear a resemblance well worth noting to the Jesus who speaks—mysteriously, invitingly, paradoxically, comfortingly, and disturbingly—in the Gospels. That similarity is perhaps made more striking when, in the latter chapters of *The Scarlet Letter*, he breaks this pattern of indirection and launches into homiletic interludes much like theatrical asides, pulling out the stops and making a forthright recommendation that the whole structure of society be "torn down and built up anew," since as it is now, it continues to retrench institutionalized injustices—to women, to outsiders, and to the children who inherit its contentions.

It is my hope that in bringing close attention to this narrator's strategies, to the ways he takes on and employs the roles of teacher, preacher, and prophet, we may come not only to a deeper understanding of Hawthorne's purposes in this remarkable little story, but also that we may recognize the ways in which its wily, accusing, inviting, forgiving narrator still speaks with surprising relevance to American readers who share the problematic legacies of those who first ventured on their "errand in the wilderness" with good hearts, very likely, but often with clouded vision, looking upon all they saw with a very human combination of hope and ambition, gratitude and greed, authentic piety, and proprietary self-justification.

What's in a Symbol

So let us begin our consideration of this narrator with one of his great prototypes, Jonathan Edwards. In "Images or Shadows of Divine Things," Edwards writes, "Roses grow upon briars, which is to signify that all temporal sweets are mixed with bitter. But what seems more especially to be meant by it is that pure happiness, the crown of glory, is to be come at in no other way than by bearing all things for Christ. The rose, that is chief of all flowers, is the last thing that comes out. The briary, prickly, bush grows before that; the end and crown of all is the beautiful and fragrant rose."[4] He goes on to inventory a number of natural objects—hills, trees, rivers, etc.—showing how each of them embodies an idea and a message, and points to God and to God's purposes. To Edwards' deeply pious and deeply allegorical sensibility, everything in the phenomenal world held a lesson from the Creator. In this he participated (brilliantly and memorably, but not altogether originally) in a long tradition of allegorical thinking, powerfully mediated for his generation by John Bunyan. Closely related to that habit of mind was typological thinking, a tradition he received fully developed from the previous two generations of Puritan theologians.

To the typological imagination, everything has meaning. Everything points beyond itself to its preexisting "type." The world and all that is in it is essentially an encoded text and our task is to learn to read it. Christian typology, an exegetical method that reads the Old Testament in terms of the New, survived in seventeenth-century-New England as a tendency to interpret history as reiteration and reaffirmation of the scriptural narratives, and to interpret every fact and incident in life as a showing forth of truths recorded in Scripture. While there is a certain richness in this habit

4. Edwards, *Images or Shadows of Divine Things*, 43.

of mind, it can easily become a self-validating safeguard against anything that threatens the dominant hermeneutical paradigm.

Charles Feidelson's classic study, *Symbolism and American Literature*,[5] helpfully traces how the writers of what F. O. Matthiessen called the "American Renaissance" (Hawthorne, Emerson, Thoreau, Melville, and their literary cohort) wrenched open that paradigm and tried with every available narrative device to entice readers to venture beyond the safe haven of allegory and into the wider, murkier, more uncertain, and more adventurous waters of symbolic thinking. Allegory stabilizes and reaffirms (the journey of Bunyan's Christian, providing, for instance, a reliable template for the Christian life); symbolism destabilizes the business of meaning making. A symbol is suggestive rather than indicative, and invites open speculation about possible meaning rather than closure and conclusiveness. Symbolism, of course, did not begin in the nineteenth century. But the way the Romantic and Transcendentalist writers in Hawthorne's New England developed symbolic thinking as a hermeneutic and an epistemology offered a radical challenge to more conventional contemporaries whose attachment to fixed meanings had narrowed their understanding of Scripture and history and diminished their imaginations.[6]

In itself the allegorical tradition is a rich one, and we still draw upon it every time we indulge in metaphor. To make meaning by seeing one thing in terms of another is almost inevitable. But to consider the possibility that, as a common adage has it, "We do not see things the way they are; we see things the way we are," opens whole new avenues of understanding and meaning making. Those inclined to greater hermeneutical caution might say it opens the broad way that leadeth to destruction. Certainly many of Hawthorne's readers would have found themselves uneasy with

---

5. Feidelson, *Symbolism and American Literature*.

6. The link between their literary purposes and the philosophical/theological thinking of Schleiermacher and Kant lies most clearly through Emerson and Ripley, both of whom left their respective pulpits and joined the "Transcendentalist Club" in an effort to widen what they experienced as a cramping narrow orthodoxy to make space for new research and speculations about psychology, intuition, and variations on the idea of "inner light." The conflicts Hawthorne would have witnessed in Salem as a boy and young man took place mainly between Congregationalists (Trinitarians) and Unitarians. His later critiques extended both to the Puritanism of his ancestors and to the liberal Unitarians of his own generation. As Joseph Schwartz points out, "That he rejected both has not often been recognized as a possibility, despite the fact that he called Calvinism a 'lump of lead' and Unitarianism 'a feather' in the same passage." Schwartz, "Three Aspects," 195.

his taste for indeterminacy. They were familiar with paradox, and knew how to wrestle with ambiguity, but the almost perverse inconclusiveness to which we are led by the narrator in *The Scarlet Letter* poses a strenuous challenge to the appetite for certainty, and to the exclusionary tendencies of those who believed they possessed it.[7]

In the introductory framing narrative, "The Custom House," the author makes clear that, though a "mere teller of tales," his object is to discern the truth precisely by employing the imagination. It is important to pause and appreciate the boldness of this position—that imagination is an instrument of discernment and an avenue of access to the truth. In a culture that regarded fiction as distracting and seductive, that itself was a radical claim. Imagination uncontrolled by reason and doctrine, after all, can easily run wild, and run readers into the "moral wilderness" in which the hapless Hester found herself at the nadir of her social career. The narrator of that introductory "history," though, unlike the narrator of the ensuing "tale," appears to be a curious and inventive, but essentially reliable historian, so we enter the tale expecting what we have learned to expect from fiction—images that lead to understanding and words that mean what they say. We are quickly disabused. In the very first chapter, the narrator abdicates his hermeneutical responsibilities. Calling our attention to a rose bush by the prison door, from which "our narrative" is about to "issue," he muses,

> This rose-bush, by a strange chance, has been kept alive in history, but whether it had merely survived out of the stern old wilderness, so long after the fall of the gigantic pines and oaks that originally overshadowed it,—or whether, as there is fair authority for believing, it had sprung up under the footsteps of the sainted Ann Hutchinson, as she entered the prison-door,—we shall not take upon us to determine.

We shall not? Why ever not? The spin on the ball he tosses to the reader here is dizzying. The question what we are to make of this rose bush suddenly becomes fraught with perplexity. It is evidently remarkably old, and that, he claims, by "strange chance," thus begging the question of cause and effect at the outset. Then we are offered two possible alternative

---

7. "In a character study, *The Man of Adamant*, that ranks in power with *Ethan Brand*, he satirizes intolerance and the exclusiveness of those who feel that they alone are the elect. This attitude, which made the saved one shrink from the contamination of mankind, was directly opposed to Hawthorne's sense of universal brotherhood." Ibid., 197.

explanations for its survival: either it is simply a natural phenomenon, anomalous, but within the realm of the biologically explicable, or it is a miraculous relic—an outward and visible sign appearing to mark and validate a spiritual event. To point out that there is "fair authority" for believing it to be the latter adds another variable to the mix: what authority? And if this narrator cannot or will not make a basic decision about this rose bush, how are we to trust his vague assurance of the "fair authority"? Furthermore, the matter of whether Anne Hutchinson is, in fact, "sainted" or rather (as there is rather weighty, if not fair, authority for conceding) a disgraced and willful heretic, is open to dispute. Yet the narrator appears to have settled that controversy without much ado, on the side of her heretical antinomianism. Intuition and indwelling grace, personal and particular revelation, appear to trump the authority of the church that banished the historical Mrs. Hutchinson from Massachusetts in 1638.

Our narrator, who appeared to be a respectable guide to colonial history in the opening paragraphs, alluding easily to known events in the early history of Boston, and who showed an appealingly philosophical turn of mind in his ruminations on the significance of prison house and burial ground as "necessities" of every human community, has slipped rapidly into a shadier role. Glancing back at the opening paragraphs we see the disturbing frequency with which he qualifies and even undermines the most ordinary observations with phrases that relieve him of responsibility for the accuracy of his account: "it may safely be assumed," "it seemed," "it looked," it was "evidently" the case. All this slippage is disconcerting. And after his inconclusive speculation on the origins of the rose-bush he feels himself suddenly compelled to "pluck one of its flowers and present it to the reader" in the hope that it will "symbolize some sweet moral blossom" to be found in this "tale of human frailty and sorrow." The moral signified, of course, remains to be determined. Or not.

This is a long way from Jonathan Edwards' serene survey of a world that testifies richly and reliably to its Creator. But it is not, if we look back, quite so far from the rabbinical ruses of Jesus, who, though he ultimately favored his disciples with explanations of his puzzling parables, offered his adversaries, and sometimes even his friends, riddles and paradoxes, inexplicable acts of mercy and sometimes lawless and incendiary guidance— instruction that often left them baffled. This is the Jesus who told those who sought to catch him out on the matter of paying taxes to the Roman state, "Render unto Caesar what is Caesar's and unto God what is God's," leaving his hearers to parse the matter of what *is*, in fact, Caesar's and what is God's. This narrator will not give us a way out of our hermeneutical responsibilities, but, as with the teacher he echoes at such distance, there is a reward waiting in his traps. To receive it, we must be willing to enlarge our patience, our tolerance for ambiguity, our minds to imagine multiple plausible possibilities, and finally our hearts to allow for radically different points of view and lines of interpretive logic than those we may hold dear.

We may not escape into hermeneutical neutrality. At every turn the narrator demands a decision, often by refusing to make one. He implies and suggests; he offers a judgment and retracts it; he poses questions that appear to be rhetorical, but may not be; he deals in double negatives; his vantage point in time and space keeps shifting, as do his sympathies, leaving us feeling, perhaps like the disciples, a little rudderless.

One feature readers accustomed to "realistic" novels often find daunting in *The Scarlet Letter* is the quality of "stiffness" in the situations and characters—the highly stylized treatment of scenes, many of which seem as static as *tableaux vivants*. We might recall, for instance, Hester standing Madonna-like on the scaffold holding Pearl, with Reverend Wilson and Arthur Dimmesdale leaning down from a balcony above and Roger Chillingworth with his Indian sidekick gazing intently at her from below, a finger raised in ambiguous gesture. Or Hester and Arthur seated on their mossy hillock in the forest confronted by Pearl who stands across the brook, her image doubled in the water below. Every scene is schematic and pictorial—"hieroglyphic," to use a term Hawthorne liked: our attention is quite deliberately drawn to elemental visual relationships: lines, shapes, colors, signature gestures—the hand over Arthur's heart, humpbacked Roger bending over his herbs, Pearl's bird-like dance, Hester's stillness within the "magic circle" that seems to take shape around her like a magnetic field. The schematic character of these scenes and figures has been called "iconic," and certainly the characters do have something in common with icons designed to serve as gateways to God that confront the viewer with curious intensity, often with what seems to be, if not accusation, at least a challenge to look into their eyes as sites of mystical encounter with both God and self.

Another technique borrowed from visual art is signification by color. Five colors form the story's limited palette: red, black, grey, green, and gold, the last two associated almost exclusively with Pearl, the "natural" child. Three archetypal sites comprise the world of the story: town, seashore, and forest, each of which imposes its own restrictions, permissions, and dangers. Elementary shapes recur repeatedly: squares, circles, and triangles, and sometimes pentagons, long associated with magic—all of which resonate with significance, though the significance may be variously read. And the four characters, different as they may seem, also echo, replicate, and mirror one another, so that any two of them may be seen as counterparts.

The intricacy of Hawthorne's sense of design extends to the way he encourages readers even to see the shapes of the letters as "hieroglyphs," and thus as pictures or maps that provide clues to meaning. Thus Hester's and Arthur's initials, A and H, offer two schematic diagrams of their little family: two supporting verticals and a dependent horizontal line—the ideal and the broken family figured forth in those simple configurations. And if you think in block letters, Roger's and Pearl's initials work in similar fashion: one missing a leg to stand on, the other with two legs, but in asymmetrical formation.

This kind of play goes on and on: with biblical allusion (consider Hester's relation to Esther); with references to Christian history (consider the relationship of Arthur's initials—AD—to those of Roger—RC—and you have a clue as to what the two might, in part, represent); with autobiographical allusions (it is no accident that Hawthorne who, as an artist among influential iconoclasts, deeply identified with the marginalized and thus, perhaps, with the suppressed feminine spirit he elevates in this story, put his own initial at the beginning of Hester's name. His interest in "the Woman Question" may have been largely fueled by his own contempt for a local culture and church in which the arts were closely constrained and suspect.

So, gradually, we are habituated to reading differently. We come to expect a world in which everything we look upon is replete with significance, but in which that significance remains for us to discern or imagine—or both, and in the process, if we consent to it, to enter into a new relationship with the world and its creatures. These literary devices are deeply and deliberately rooted in theological methods. They compel us to reflect on the relationship of nature to culture, natural revelation to scriptural revelation, human intention to predestination, and perhaps most strikingly, on how we interpret the world and the word. It would seem that the Reformation principle of the priesthood of all believers may have opened a Pandora's box of possibilities; and whether the multiplicity of possible meanings in signs and symbols and images and shadows be a flowering (good) or a fragmentation (bad) he shall not, apparently, take it upon himself to determine.

A few examples may serve here to show how pervasive and insistent is the narrator's invitation to the reader to pass no image or visual detail without assigning significance. Consider the frequency with which he describes the location and configuration of characters. When Roger first appears, standing by an Indian on the "outskirts of the crowd," it couldn't be plainer that, though we don't know him yet, who he is may be understood by his marginality and his alliance with an alien and suspicious outsider. Elevation is almost always an ironic reference to the hierarchical thinking that assigned what we are invited to recognize as specious priority. So when the two ministers gaze down at Hester, the immediately ensuing description of her as very like the divine Mother and Child casts their authority into question.

Similarly, when Mistress Hibbens, the local witch, calls to Hester from an upper window in her brother's (!), Governor Bellingham's, mansion, an ironic parity is implied between her knowledge, or authority, and his. When Roger, the dark physician, stands over the prone and sleeping Arthur to part his garments and peer at his chest, we recognize one of many visual comments on the relationship of scientific privilege and knowledge to religious authority and mystery. Or when Pearl stands (as she does more than once) in or by a pool, looking down at the perfect image reflected there, we begin to understand how the strange fullness of her character may come from her unimpeded relationship with her own "shadow" or, as our narrator would have it, "spiritual" self. Light and dark intermingle in her, as do what we call human and what our narrator, rather ponderously, keeps referring to as "preternatural."

Or consider the semiotics of color. References to "the Black Man" in the forest, a term borrowed from early Puritan usage to designate the devil (with obvious racist overtones that were likely unconscious to most who used it) bring both Arthur and Roger, figures we might like to polarize as good and evil, into association with him, since both go clad in black. The red of Hester's letter is echoed in the bright reds she chooses for Pearl's clothing, in the red of the roses at both the prison door and at the door of the Governor's mansion, the red letter that appears in the night sky, the red of the rising sun on Arthur's brow, and again in the "red" that describes the Indians who emerge silently from the forest at intervals throughout the story. Linked in this way, the color becomes a thread connecting apparently opposed figures and forces and suggesting some deep similarity among them. That Pearl is associated with green—in the seaweed she drapes upon herself (in the shape of an A), and in the forest mosses and sea grasses that surround her—reinforces the idea that she is a child of nature (which our narrator variously describes as "imp," "fairy," "elf," or "bird") and that her remarkable awareness and knowledge have their source in the untaught and instinctive animal world. Her answer to the Governor's catechism question, "Who made thee?" is indicative of the kind of truth she embodies: she answers "that she had not been made at all, but had been plucked by her mother off the bush of wild roses that grew by the prison door." The answer is fanciful (and our fickle narrator hastens to explain it away as such), but carries a level of symbolic truth that recalls the wisdom of dreams and visions over which the rational, taught mind has no governance. Gold, like black, serves ironically to associate Hester, whose letter is embroidered in fantastic flourishes of gold stitchery, and Pearl, who is often located in a spot of gold sunlight, and whom the sunbeams seem to follow, with the Governor, who wears gold as a sign of office and wealth.

Shapes have similar sign value. The "steeple-crowned hats" of the men in the opening sentence replicate the long, sharp vertical triangles of the New England steeple churches—a shape that is replicated, again ironically, in the A on Hester's breast and the A in Arthur's name. Indeed, the entire stage of the drama takes place in the triangle demarcated by town, seashore, and forest, and of course a love triangle of sorts gives shape to the plot. Rectangles—the town square, the prison cell, the scaffold, the burial ground, the rooms in houses, and the village square that separates prison from church—and the straight wheel tracks that connect them, remind us of all that is imposed upon the wilder, irregular shapes of nature by the hand of regulating man. Circles, on the other hand, are associated with mystery, magic, and the feminine. That Hester appears on more than one occasion to stand in a "magic circle" associates her both with the circles of women who gathered in covens outside the purview of patriarchal law, and with the "halo" of sunlight that seems at times to protect Pearl, and to set them both apart from the culture that lives on different terms in its boxes and lines and squares.

The shapes of letters we have already mentioned, but not the kinds of wordplay that invite us to look *at* words rather than through them to find new layers of meaning. Like Shakespeare, Hawthorne loved wordplay and turned all kinds of wordplay—puns, allusions, alliterations—to his own devious purposes. Those purposes, let us remember, all have to do with the question of how we get at what is true, how we interpret what is given to us to fathom, and, centrally, how we are to understand the intent of revelation in Scripture, in nature, and in the impulses of the human heart. When we read, therefore, that Pearl played in "unadulterated sunshine," it is hard to miss the imbedded reference to adultery, a word that never occurs openly in the text. That Pearl is the object of pure blessing in that moment, throws the view of her as a "living symbol of sin" into serious question. Pearl's name works at several levels of allusion. The most obvious is that spelled out by the narrator:

> Pearl!—for so had Hester called her; not as a name expressive of her aspect, which had nothing of the calm, white, unimpassioned lustre that would be indicated by the comparison. But she named the infant "Pearl," as being of great price—purchased with all she had—her mother's only treasure!

Characteristically, the narrator points out (for those of us who, like dull disciples, might easily miss the point) the curious misfit between Pearl's name and her comportment, and directs us to another level of quite plausible and appropriate meaning. Later, though, when Governor Bellingham objects that she should be called "Ruby, rather!—or Coral!—or Red Rose," we are subtly redirected to biological comparisons that might remind us that a pearl is created in the body of the oyster in an effort to protect itself from an extraneous irritant that has entered its soft interior. Hmm. It appears there is meaning here, as well—another illustration of the ways in which different systems of reference may yield different meanings.

One other instance of wordplay may suffice here to make the point about its importance for Hawthorne. At his first appearance in the town, Roger Chillingworth explains his arrival to a stranger by claiming that he was "brought hither by this Indian to be redeemed out of my captivity." The historical accuracy of the term is clear: it was not uncommon for European colonists to be captured in the course of land disputes with nearby native tribes, and to have to pay ransom for their return. Indeed, so-called "captivity narratives" became so popular as to be conventionalized in the late eighteenth century, and that they ended with "redemption" made it easy to incorporate these distressing invasions into the governing typological narratives by which they elaborately justified their settlement on tribal lands. But Roger, in this same scene, appears to have lingered in captivity and adapted rather thoroughly to Indian ways. He is, our narrator tells us, "clad in a strange disarray of civilized and savage costume." As we soon learn, he has learned much of what he knows and practices from the Indians. So the idea of his "redemption" from a dark and sinful place, from the Indian encampment as a prototype of hell, doesn't quite work. In fact this description and others tend to deconstruct the simplistic polarities subsequent generations tended to adopt in considering the relations between "white men" and "savages." And certainly it deconstructs, in its use of the word "redeem" the too easy association of historical circumstances with legitimating biblical prototypes.

Though the narrator often invokes allegorical and typological thinking, for instance in observing that Pearl "was a forcible type, in [her] little frame, of the moral agony which Hester Prynne had borne," he invariably offers alternative ways of seeing and interpreting. In describing the child in her pursuit of the Puritan children who torment her as resembling "an infant pestilence—the scarlet fever, or some such half-fledged angel of judgment—whose mission was to punish the sins of the rising generation," he subverts the power of these associations by insinuating that the opposite is also true. Pearl, for instance, is also an agent of truth in the insistent and inconvenient questions that drive to the heart of her parents' secrets: "What does the letter mean, mother? and why dost thou wear it? and why does the minister keep his hand over his heart?" Her questions keep the adults accountable and force moral decisions, as when she asks Arthur, who has acknowledged her in the secrecy of the forest, "But wilt thou promise . . . to take my hand, and mother's hand, to-morrow noon-tide?" So we are left to ponder whether she is a sign of sin or an agent of grace—and of course, we can only really conclude that she is both.

But there is more. The narrator takes us beyond the paradox that this strange little girl child may represent both good and evil. That Pearl looks "like a wild tropical bird of rich plumage, ready to take flight into the upper air" suggests that there is about her something that doesn't readily submit to moral categories, and that something mysterious and lovely about her character (and that of any child still uncorrupted by too much civilizing) defies easy judgment. Indeed, the repetition of "wild" (a word that occurs sixty-seven times in the story) serves to remind us that the natural, uncultivated world both around us and within us, the realm of instincts, intuitions, and dreams, may not submit to the moral categories we tend to impose upon our own behavior. Even if we concede that nature is "fallen," we are left to wonder in what sense, since nature seems also to be a vehicle of revelation and divine beneficence. The natural world in *The Scarlet Letter*, with its sympathetic sun that makes haloes and lights paths and its dark grasses that testify to the evils of the dead seems to have something in common with the "nature" the Psalmist describes where the rocks and hills rejoice and clap their hands. And so Pearl's association with nature raises the question of how to think about the behavior and training of children: what damage do we do in tampering with their "natural" instincts and dividing what seems to be a wholeness of body, mind, and soul not yet drawn into the suffering of self-awareness? That this wholeness is a feature of Pearl's being and appearance is made plain in passages like this one, from chapter 21:

> The dress, so proper was it to little Pearl, seemed an effluence, or inevitable development and outward manifestation of her charac-ter, no more to be separated from her than the many-hued bril-liancy from a butterfly's wing, or the painted glory from the leaf of a bright flower. As with these, so with the child; her garb was all of one idea with her nature.

She is all of a piece, at one with herself: her clothing, her character, her variegated emotional register, her intuitions and her actions converge in unimpeded instinctual response to something deeply true, but unnamed and undisclosed. Thus we are led to consider "wildness" not as something to be tamed, but as something to be valued and recovered. Hawthorne echoes a note here that sounds more radically and explicitly in Thoreau's famous dictum, "In wildness is the salvation of the world." If one takes that not as a theological proposition, but at least as an insistence upon the importance of stewarding rightly a gift left precariously in our hands, these invitations to reflect on "the wild" seem consequential, indeed.

A similar ambiguity leads us repeatedly to reconsider allegorical equations and conventional judgments suggested by Roger's humpback (deformity of body suggesting deformity of soul) or by the round, ruddy, bold, and hard-featured bodies of the Puritan women whose "moral diet" the narrator points out, was "not a whit more refined" than the beef and ale their recent ancestors consumed. Arthur's tremulous voice and Hester's tall stature and shining hair invite us to recognize their respective sensi-tivity, strength, and beauty; Rev. Wilson's beard, his venerability; Mistress

Hibbens' cackle, her witchcraft. But all of these characters are held up for further scrutiny that modifies and sometimes overturns our initial judgments. Though Roger begins as a kind of naturalized half-breed, neither fish nor fowl, and thus socially suspect, and though he is rather relentlessly shackled to satanic imagery in the final chapters—a lurid gleam in his eye, an infernal glance, a snakelike approach—it is also he whose remarkable acts of mercy frame the story. He alone visits Hester in prison and cares for her sick child. And in the end, he leaves to Pearl, the illegitimate child of his wife's infidelity, all his fortune, enabling her to escape the narrow judgments of the townspeople and return to Europe, from whence she sends her mother gifts "which only wealth could have purchased and affection have imagined." This last telling comment on Pearl's lavish gratitude for the wayward mother who raised her at the margins seems a pointed affirmation of the goodness of worldly pleasures and of love that has learned to be extravagant (in the deepest sense) and unstinting.

Though Arthur seems to betray Hester with his silence throughout the story, his own suffering, the power of his sermons, the piety he inspires, and the ways he cares for the town's spiritual welfare at his own expense, must make us wonder whether the justice of full public confession might be too simple a thing to insist on. And Hester, wronged though she is, is not in all respects ennobled by her suffering and penance. In "Another View of Hester," at the very heart of the story, the narrator inventories her losses: she has become embittered; she has lost something of her womanliness, her capacity for natural affections, her interest in life itself. She has "wandered in a moral wilderness" so long as to become literally bewildered, and has no "moral compass." And though in the end she appears as a wisdom figure, teaching young women what costly experience has taught her, and though she chooses a path of humility and sacrifice, we are required to ask to what extent her spiritual gains represent a kind of Pyrrhic victory.

Thus, in one ambiguity after another, our narrator trains us in negative capability[8]—that virtue of the poetic mind that enables it to entertain ambiguity and paradox without "straining after resolution." The truths

---

8. This term, coined by the poet John Keats, puts a name to an essential tenet of Romanticism—that truth does not finally submit to the terms of rational discourse or linguistic constructions, but demands a sustained dialogue between the subjective and objective mind—or between fact and fancy—and language that preserves the tension between them.

he has to impart cannot be told without paradox. The grey that Hester wears might surely serve to remind us of the grey area we all inhabit. And that reminder might serve as a warning to readers inclined to rush to judgment that true discernment remembers that we see through a glass darkly, that the logs in our own eyes impede our vision, and that we are in no position, finally, to judge. The images and shadows of divine things that surround us, and even the words we speak, are multifarious, multivalent, multifaceted points in a shifting field where truths may be constellated as clearly as the "A" that shines in Arthur's night sky, and still remain ambiguous. It is the character of revelation and of wisdom, he teaches us, to lead us to the threshold of mystery and require that we bow there before what cannot be known or spoken.

Again and again the writer's message is that words do not work to a single purpose, or only indicatively, but poetically, performatively, associatively, speculatively, pictorially, inviting us to dwell (as Emily Dickinson puts it) in possibility, "a fairer house than prose." It is a fairer house because it is a place where play is permitted, where multiple meanings may coexist, where negative capability is a kind of courtesy—ambiguity is embraced and paradox a source of delight. Literalists will shun this house of pleasure and condemn it as a palace of sin, but, as our narrator might put it, there is fair evidence for believing that in its mystery and diversity and lively, fluid, even perichoretic, way of dancing with words, this house may be one of the "many mansions" in the Kingdom of Heaven.

Part II

—✝—

Scriptures
Reconsidered

-1-

Judge Not

*Judge not, that ye be not judged. For with what judgment
ye judge, ye shall be judged: and with what measure ye mete,
it shall be measured to you again.*

MATTHEW 7:1–2

FEW WHO HAVE READ *The Scarlet Letter* will forget the opening scene of chapter 2 where Hester Prynne, her baby in her arms, makes her slow way through a heckling crowd from the prison to the scaffold. The most vocal among her critics are women. One insists, "We women, being of mature age and church-members in good repute should have the handling of such malefactresses as this Hester Prynne," since the men in charge of her sentencing are "merciful overmuch." One suggests a "brand of hot iron" as a suitable penance for Hester's crime. Another, whom our unabashed narrator describes as "the ugliest as well as the most pitiless of these self-constituted judges," takes the logic of punishment to its extreme: "This woman has brought shame upon us all, and ought to die. Is there not law for it? Truly there is, both in the Scripture and the statute-book. Then let the magistrates, who have made it of no effect, thank themselves if their own wives and daughters go astray!"

Who are these women? And, perhaps more to the point, who do they think they are? The narrator describes them unflatteringly as near descendants of the "man-like Elizabeth," with "broad shoulders and well-developed busts," and "round and ruddy cheeks" whose "boldness and rotundity of speech" matched their "not unsubstantial persons." They were women, he claims, of a "coarser fiber" than the "fair descendents" likely to be reading his tale. One is a "hard-featured dame of fifty," another an "autumnal matron," and a third conspicuously ugly as well as pitiless. The acerbic and misogynistic description itself visits such harsh judgment on the women that one is tempted, at least if one is a female reader, to rush to their defense. In their sexless, aging androgyny they evoke some memory of Macbeth's three witches—mockeries of all that is feminine, whatever that may be. Like Lady Macbeth they seem to have been "unsexed" and hardened by a driving force as strong as her vaulting ambition. Yet it is hard to align oneself fully with the scorn of a narrator so inclined to regard age and unloveliness as morally offensive.

Like every scene in this incessantly ambiguous tale, this one involves the reader in a dilemma: whether to accept the judgments of a fickle narrator who seems to have a privileged vantage point, but whose high moral ground seems seismically unstable, or to resist those judgments out of sympathy with the objects of his scorn. Our sympathies very likely shift, and with them the reasoning by which we arrive at our own assessments of the various characters. Certainly the women are not particularly appealing: they are crude, harsh, self-righteous, and take wicked delight in another's shame. Yet even as the narrator offers them up as objects of mockery, the judgments we are invited to pass may strike us as unjust—not entirely unlike those of the women themselves.

Our judgments continue to be invited and challenged on every page by our whimsical, cunning narrator, who freely passes judgment upon one character after another, shifting perspectives and conclusions as the story goes on. At times he seems to align himself with the authorities' view of Hester, at other times with her own view of herself. He teases us into making judgments we are later compelled to modify, retract, or suspend. This trickery subverts any effort we might make to affirm our predispositions or prejudices by adopting a single point of view. His insistence on multiple perspectives drives the point home that we are never in a position to render a wholly just judgment. In his subversion of conventional narrative authority and reliability, Hawthorne leads us to concede the impossibility of unassailable and reliable judgment on the part of any mere human. Thus the story becomes a parable about the consequences of judging where we have been enjoined by divine ordinance to "judge not." Helpfully, it provides his troubled readers with a number of reasons why passing moral judgment is a bad idea.

In the opening scene where the women judge Hester, we see the first of his unsettling warnings to those who make it their business to blame: judgment makes you ugly. It deforms you. The women who pass judgment on Hester appear to be manlike, withered, and ugly. Before we leap to our own judgments about the author's offensive attitude toward women, age, and fat, we might recall that bodies, like every other image in this narrative, are symbolic. By the logic of symbols, consistent throughout the book, every object, space, and person in the novel is a morally charged signifier. Thus in the logic of Hawthorne's characterization, the body is literally, as St. Thomas put it, the "form of the soul." What is external manifests what is internal. Age and ugliness, loss of womanliness in women, can be traced to the attitudes that deformed them. We don't need to take this equation literally to take its spiritual and psychological meaning.

Yet neither is the story simple allegory; images don't carry fixed meaning, and the ambiguities of character invite us to speculate rather freely about what psychological or spiritual truths they may embody: we must at least wonder, for instance, how these women got that way. What makes them so merciless that their hardness has been recorded in the very tissues of their bodies? There are some obvious possibilities: they are genuinely horrified at the sin of adultery; they are jealous of Hester's youth and beauty; every time someone else is punished, the load of their own personal guilt is lightened by relief that they have been passed by once more by the avenging angel; they need the negative bond of a common object of scorn to insure their own sense of community and safety. Perhaps the only terms on which they can insure female community in a stringent patriarchy are terms that appear to corroborate patriarchal authority. So though they share Hester's vulnerability as women without authority or status who live at the will of the men who rule over them, when they align themselves with those rulers, they secure their own safety.

All of these reasons factor, no doubt, into their behavior, strikingly reminiscent of the fickle crowd in the Gospel story prepared to stone the woman caught in adultery. The parallel to that biblical scene is pointed enough to suggest that this is a community whose Christianity

has become exactly as corrupt in its degenerate piety as the faith of the
Pharisees. As modern-day counterparts to those objects of Jesus' contempt, the members of this community are subject to the same judgments
Jesus pronounced on them: "Woe unto you scribes and Pharisees, hypo-
crites!" They have fallen into the same trap of self-serving religiosity, and
their righteousness is like the "filthy rags" to which Isaiah compares it.
Ironically those "filthy rags" refer in Hebrew to rags covered with men-
strual blood—an image clearly linking sin to womanhood. These women
have, as the narrator implies, divulged the dark side of womanhood by accepting the judgments the culture lays on them and displacing them onto
an available scapegoat. The process invalidates their piety and destroys
what is most humane about them. They are hoisted on their own petard.

A second warning against the presumption of those who set themselves up to judge others comes in the introduction of the Reverend John
Wilson, "the eldest clergyman of Boston, a great scholar, like most of his
contemporaries in the profession, and withal a man of kind and genial
spirit." Typically, what the narrator gives with one hand he again takes
with the other: immediately upon mention of Wilson's "kind and genial
spirit," he adds a sharp and skeptical note: "This last attribute, however,
had been less carefully developed than his intellectual gifts, and was,
in truth, rather a matter of shame than self-congratulation with him."
Reiterated in the development of both Roger's and Arthur's characters,
the notion that intellectual gifts are at best a dangerous, morally precarious endowment points strongly to Jesus' own challenges to the learned
and the clever who spun the law to their own purposes, rationalizing their
prejudices in ways that reinforced their political power. In them, and in
the leaders of the Puritan theocracy, we see how the law becomes an agent
of condemnation rather than of spiritual and political health, and an instrument of self-protection in the hands of the clever. The narrator, in one
of his own frequent judgmental moments, identifies Wilson as one who
has been so long sequestered in the isolation of a dark study, peering into
books instead of human faces, that he "looked like the darkly engraved
portraits which we see prefixed to old volumes of sermons, and had no
more right than one of those portraits would have to step forth, as he now
did, and meddle with a question of human guilt, passion, and anguish."
Intellectual preoccupation has isolated him from lived relationship with
a living community, and that isolation fosters in him the delusion that,
knowing more than most, he is in a position to judge others. Judgment, in

his case, distilled from theological abstractions alone rather than emerging organically from the affective complexity of human relationship, becomes an instrument of death rather than of life. Kind as he seems to be, he is willing to sacrifice the beauty, promise, and hope of at least two young lives to abstract principle. The principle itself has merit: sin must be exposed, named, and its consequences made manifest for the sake of the community. But in practice, human forms of punishment mostly fail to reform, as any history of prisons and penalties will show. Hewing to principle in this way does not enhance and protect the life of the community, but rather retrenches an ethic of fear, blame, and secrecy.

In Governor Bellingham, as in the Reverend Wilson, we are invited to take a hard look at the institutions of power that elevate a few to the precarious position of judge over others. Like the Reverend Wilson's, Governor Bellingham's character seems largely a function of his role: his job is to adjudicate Hester's worthiness to keep and raise her child:

> Among those who promoted the design, Governor Bellingham was said to be one of the most busy. It may appear singular, and indeed, not a little ludicrous, that an affair of this kind, which in later days would have been referred to no higher jurisdiction than that of the select men of the town, should then have been a question publicly discussed, and on which statesmen of eminence took sides. At that epoch of pristine simplicity, however, matters of even slighter public interest, and of far less intrinsic weight than the welfare of Hester and her child, were strangely mixed up with the deliberations of legislators and acts of state. The period was hardly, if at all, earlier than that of our story, when a dispute concerning the right of property in a pig not only caused a fierce and bitter contest in the legislative body of the colony, but resulted in an important modification of the framework itself of the legislature.

The point could hardly be clearer: institutionalizing judgment leads to presumption, pettiness, loss of perspective, and often to ludicrous and foolish assignment of disproportionate importance to drivel. It consumes the energies of a community in matters that distract them from their real spiritual and political welfare.

Perhaps no single scene in the novel is more comic than the one in which Governor Bellingham attempts to render judgment on Pearl's upbringing and Hester's fitness by posing questions from the Westminster Catechism. In comparison to her fanciful, sprightly, and surprising answers, in which truths of remarkable psychological depth are embedded in a language of symbols, his flat-footed efforts to extract rote and lit-eral responses appear not only ridiculous, but pathetic. Though he may believe in the righteousness of his intentions, his frame of reference is formulaic, unimaginative, and sharply reminiscent of Jesus' warning that the letter of the law kills, but the Spirit gives life.

The figure of Roger Chillingworth, another learned male who bears yet another kind of social authority as physician, provides us with another argument against judgment: it is a sickness. Like an aggressive cancer, it overtakes and kills one's healthier spiritual capacities and habits of mind—compassion, imagination, common sense, forgiveness, love. Our very first introduction to him presents him as the one person in the community who has ventured to dwell with and learn from the native peoples—a fact that at the time would surely cast some shadow upon his character, though twenty-first-century readers will mostly find this a point in his favor. Shortly thereafter the jailer describes him as "a man of skill in all Christian modes of physical science, and likewise familiar with whatever the savage people could teach in respect to medicinal herbs and roots that grew in the forest." He is, then, a genuinely curious, culturally open and competent healer, who alone, among the reticent townspeople, comes to visit Hester in prison.

Surprisingly, Roger does not condemn his erring wife, but treats her with remarkable forgiveness upon their reunion in her prison cell, and even concedes his own role in bringing about her downfall. He en-ters her cell quietly and turns his attention first of all to her crying baby. When Hester hesitates to give Pearl the medicine he offers, he rebukes her, reasonably enough, on grounds of common sense: "Foolish woman! . . . What should ail me to harm this misbegotten and miserable babe?" Clearly, these early ministrations are grounded in a solid medical ethic of doing no harm that Roger himself seems to identify with both common sense and mental health. Then he offers Hester a sedative potion, once again rebuking her suspicions that he might be offering poison: "Dost thou know me so little, Hester Prynne? Are my purposes wont to be so shallow? Even if I imagine a scheme of vengeance, what could I do better for my object than to let thee live . . . so that this burning shame may still blaze upon thy bosom?" Though the dark possibility of prolonging her shame modifies his kindlier intentions, Roger speaks at this point as a reasonable man, capable of kindness, if not yet of whole-hearted forgiveness. Indeed, in a moment that gives the reader a fair measure of his native wisdom and fair-mindedness, he speaks generously to the wife who has betrayed him:

> I ask not wherefore, nor how thou hast fallen into the pit, or say rather, thou hast ascended to the pedestal of infamy on which I found thee. The reason is not far to seek. It was my folly, and thy weakness. I—a man of thought—the book-worm of great libraries —a man already in decay, having given my best years to feed the hungry dream of knowledge—what had I to do with youth and beauty like thine own? Misshapen from my youth, how could I de-lude myself with the idea that intellectual gifts might veil physical deformity in a young girl's fantasy? Men call me wise. If sages were ever wise in their own behoof, I might have foreseen all this.

The speech itself offers evidence of the wisdom others have attributed to him. Though he does not deny the seriousness of Hester's sin, he takes full responsibility for helping to create the conditions that led to it. That sin is a shared condition—that sins take place in entrapping social systems and are often a function of assigned roles—is a recurrent theme in the story, articulated most clearly here by the character who ultimately seems most deeply implicated.

Roger's wisdom, however, and the spiritual and mental health he ex-hibits in this early scene, are gradually eroded and destroyed by his com-pulsive fixation on Arthur as the perpetrator of the "crime" for which he so generously excuses Hester. At first, making Arthur a scapegoat seems to enable him to deal with Hester more generously. But his capacity for generosity falls short of similarly imagining Arthur's lonely circumstances —his confusion, his youthful needs, his passion. Rather he renders an early and unwavering judgment that not only subverts and perverts his healing work, but fatally afflicts his own soul and body. What begins as a reasonable desire to expose the adulterer and make him share Hester's punishment gradually becomes an obsession. Judgment overtakes all other motives and drives out the compassion of which we have seen him to be capable. His capacity to recognize his own complicity in fault makes his ultimate descent into obsession the more tragic.

As the story progresses, the imagery associated with Roger—the "lurid gleam" of his eye, the deformity of his body, and the satanic quali-ties that appear more insistently and overtly in the final chapters ("per-haps, so dark, disturbed, and evil was his look, he rose up out of some nether region")—leaves us little choice but to recognize the pathological consequences of his driving need to judge and convict one who has, ironically, become his patient, his intimate, and his intellectual companion.

The pathos and touching suggestiveness of Roger's leaving his entire estate to Pearl underscore what is vestigially and pathetically humane even in this deeply corrupted figure who dies consumed by his own Faustian rage for a moral order he can control and comprehend. Though presuming to judge others has been his undoing, the quality of mercy survives even the ravages of his cankerous obsession—a testimony to mercy and grace that outlives the worst of human sinfulness.

Perhaps the most poignant message about the dangers of presuming to judge where only God can see is delivered in the chronicles of Arthur's and Hester's tormented interior lives. In both cases, self-judgment is their undoing—in Arthur's case, fatally so. Hester survives the ravages of self-judgment to the extent that she is finally able to extricate herself from the constraints of a church that has, in any case, excluded her and refused the nurturing, forgiveness, or compassion one might have hoped it would purvey. But to the extent that both she and Arthur internalize the rigid Calvinistic moral code by which they are judged, they become incapable of authentic, flexible, lively human relationship. Self-judgment isolates and strangulates souls that were made to flourish in beloved community.

Readers are often tempted to render their own harsh judgments of Arthur for his evident hypocrisy in failing to come forward and claim his share of punishment. But Arthur's case is not so simple. As pastor, his designated duty is, as his elders remind him, to care for his parishioners' souls—including that of the young woman who stands before him. The long history of sexual misconduct among church leaders offers ambiguous guidance at best about when exposure serves the best spiritual interests of the community. A case can at least be made that Arthur is doing his best to carry out his duty as spiritual leader by bearing his guilt in private rather than exposing the weaker ones in his flock to scandal, disillusionment, and loss of faith. Whether or not one is inclined to take this sanguine view of his obligations, it may serve to make his anguish more comprehensible. Perhaps the best we can say for Arthur is that he is a victim of his own scruples—and both Catholic and Protestant traditions teach that scrupulosity, or anxious moral quibbling, is a form of spiritual sickness that ignores the benevolence and forefends the healing action of divine grace. Whatever psychosomatic illness or disfigurement we may attribute to Arthur's long, slow struggle to bear his secret shame with some integrity—and we are left, as mentioned above, tantalizingly in the dark about the diagnosis—it becomes increasingly clear that the relentless guilt produced by his self-judgment is, more than anything else, the cause of his death.

As in Roger's case, so also in Arthur's, however, shafts of grace penetrate even the dark thickets of obsession. In one of the most theologically provocative and deeply hopeful passages in the novel, Arthur, desperately resisting Roger's persistent efforts to get him to confess his secret sin, confesses instead his last, best hope not only in the mercy, but in the judgment of God, the only one capable of judging the secrets of the human heart:

> There can be, if I forbode aright, no power, short of the Divine mercy, to disclose, whether by uttered words, or by type or emblem, the secrets that may be buried in the human heart. The heart, making itself guilty of such secrets, must perforce hold them, until the day when all hidden things shall be revealed. Nor have I so read or interpreted Holy Writ, as to understand that the disclosure of human thoughts and deeds, then to be made, is intended as a part of the retribution. That, surely, were a shallow view of it. No; these revelations, unless I greatly err, are meant merely to promote the intellectual satisfaction of all intelligent beings, who will stand waiting, on that day, to see the dark problem of this life made plain. A knowledge of men's hearts will be needful to the completest solution of that problem. And I conceive, moreover, that the hearts holding such miserable secrets as you speak of, will yield them up, at that last day, not with reluctance, but with a joy unutterable.

In this speech, where fine thought and equally fine feeling come together, we encounter the most positive and theologically satisfying reason to withhold or at least bracket human judgment. Divine judgment is likely to be more generous, more truly righteous, more intellectually satisfying, and tempered by more—indeed infinite—mercy than any human judgment that might be rendered. It is an argument, perhaps, against the human institutions that preserve accountability by exposing crime and folly to the public eye. Much might be argued on both sides of the problem of crime and suitable punishment. Our fallen state in which a prison is "among the earliest practical necessities" to be erected in any new settlement seems to make unsatisfying conclusions and partial justice inevitable. But Arthur's point here, not to be missed, is that just judgment is not a thing to dread, but to look forward to. God's judgment, as he imagines it, is a source of relief and renewal—even before the balm of mercy that will surely accompany it.

An interesting effect of Arthur's predicament is the intensified eloquence that becomes, ironically, a gift that seems to mark him as a prophetic figure within the community. Out of his own woundedness comes a gift for others. This, too, Hawthorne seems to imply, is the way of the Lord: from Moses to Jonah to Paul to Augustine, bearers of God's message of mercy have often been those most in need of it. Insofar as Arthur's self-judgment produces actual humility rather than sordid humiliation, he becomes more aware of the truth that sin is a shared condition of humankind, less inclined to judge his fellow sinners, and more deeply motivated to speak to them in ways that free them from the shackles of the judgment he suffers.

Like Arthur's, Hester's self-judgment seems, at least for a time, to turn her inward and cut her off from the nourishments of human kindness. But her position and temperament are different from his. Though she suffers, she survives in part by the resiliency that enables her to take refuge outside the church in the "moral wilderness." She dwells there at considerable cost:

> All the light and graceful foliage of her character had been withered up by this red-hot brand, and had long ago fallen away, leaving a bare and harsh outline, which might have been repulsive had she possessed friends or companions to be repelled by it. Even the attractiveness of her person had undergone a similar change. It might be partly owing to the studied austerity of her dress, and partly to the lack of demonstration in her manners.... It was due in part to all these causes, but still more to something else, that there seemed to be no longer anything in Hester's face for Love to dwell upon; nothing in Hester's form, though majestic and statue like, that Passion would ever dream of clasping in its embrace; nothing in Hester's bosom to make it ever again the pillow of Affection. Some attribute had departed from her, the permanence of which had been essential to keep her a woman. Such is frequently the fate and such the stern development, of the feminine character and person, when the woman has encountered, and lived through, an experience of peculiar severity. If she be all tenderness, she will die. If she survive, the tenderness will either be crushed out of her, or—and the outward semblance is the same—crushed so deeply into her heart that it can never show itself more.

The warning here is clear: self-judgment, so often the internalized judgment of others more powerful and socially accredited, leads to self-doubt, self-betrayal, self-shaming, and loss of connection with the One who calls us into life and sustains us in it. But along with this warning comes a new avenue of hope. In the second half of the book, we see a new Hester emerging—a woman empowered in her heterodoxy, who has accepted her alienation from the structures of church and state, and lives in the "moral wilderness" of her own mind and heart as well as in the actual wilderness outside the town. It is not a hope Hawthorne's readers would easily have embraced, coming as it does with a forceful indictment of the institutional church. Still, it seems that Hester, who at the end of the book appears as a Christ-like figure, dispensing hard-won wisdom to a circle of female disciples, holds out the promise of anti-institutional salvation outside the church that has forsaken its own roots in shared life and intimate relational commitments like those of the early Christian communities.

This scene, in the chapter entitled "Another View of Hester," that lies at the geographic center of the story, represents a nadir in her spiritual life, but also a beginning: in a move whose ironic power is the equal of any of the narrator's stratagems, Hester accomplishes a complete inversion of her punishment. What has been an instrument of shame becomes a token of pride. The judgments visited upon her are one by one retracted, as she not only lives down, but lives beyond them, into a moral realm where she is beyond social control. She comes to a point where she "scorns" to consider the approbation of the townspeople desirable, and lives outside the reach of their judgments. In this the narrator likens her to the Reformers:

> The world's law was no law for her mind. It was an age in which the human intellect, newly emancipated, had taken a more active and a wider range than for many centuries before. Men of the sword had overthrown nobles and kings. Men bolder than these had overthrown and rearranged—not actually, but within the sphere of theory, which was their most real abode—the whole system of ancient prejudice, wherewith was linked much of ancient principle. Hester Prynne imbibed this spirit. She assumed a freedom of speculation, then common enough on the other side of the Atlantic, but which our forefathers, had they known it, would have held to be a deadlier crime than that stigmatised by the scarlet letter. In her lonesome cottage, by the seashore, thoughts visited her such as dared to enter no other dwelling in New England; shadowy guests,

that would have been as perilous as demons to their entertainer, could they have been seen so much as knocking at her door.

Good can come of evil. The judgments that burn away Hester's "womanly" softness drive her to claim her life in new and heroic ways. The sacrifice of her "femininity" makes way for a new and potent kind of womanhood. Hawthorne's own notorious ambivalence about strong and independent women makes this portrait of an emergent "new woman" interestingly two-edged. Escaping the role that inheres in belittling notions of femininity, she enlarges into a space previously inaccessible. Her story, ending as it does with the adulterous woman as healer, mother, teacher, and wisdom figure, implicitly poses readers the question, "Are you ready for this?" Are you ready to recognize goodness in empowering the very people you feel need to be controlled?

The scriptural admonition to "judge not" comes with a warning: your judgments will come back to haunt you. You will be held to your own harsh standards and found wanting. Hawthorne amplifies this warning throughout this post-Reformation parable: if you presume to pass judgment upon others without knowing their stories, without access to their secrets, without the eyes of compassion, without a recognition of shared sinfulness, and certainly without the God's eye view that no one on earth can have, your judgments will diminish you; they will make you sick and ugly and deformed; they will drive you to defeat your own best purposes; they will injure both the Body of Christ and the body politic. Grace is the only answer to this predicament—grace recognized, and extended, and received. It is the church's shame that it has not always been an agent of the grace it proclaims. Certainly in this story it falls far short of that high calling. But grace of its own kind is available in nature, in the love of a child for her pariah parent, in loyalty born of authentic mutual love, and in the gratitude that grows and flourishes where mercy survives among the weeds of harsh human "justice."

-2-

Not By Bread Alone

*Man shall not live by bread alone, but by every word
that proceedeth out of the mouth of God.*

MATTHEW 4:4

THE ANCIENT HEBREWS REGARDED utterance as a sacred gift: every
spoken word was shaped and borne on the breath of life, each breath
a gift of Spirit.[1] A high view of language is essential not only to Judeo-
Christian tradition, but to every faith tradition, not to mention the many
who claim no faith but find in story, song, poetry, or simply conversation
something essential and life-giving.

Paradoxically, though, the more we attend to language, the more we
find ourselves involved in the "wrestle with words and meanings" that
Eliot bemoaned and Joyce celebrated. Whether that wrestling is, like
Jacob's with the angel, a desperate attempt to survive a divine encounter,
or a playful engagement with possibility, we need not, as Hawthorne's
narrator might put it, "take upon ourselves to determine." In either case
the fact remains that words "slip, slide, perish, decay with imprecision, /

---

1. See Barry Sanders' explanation of this point in *A is for Ox*, 57.

35

will not stay in place, will not stay still."[2] Hawthorne knew this, and made the point a century before Eliot did, and left his stamp on the long legacy of vigorous ambiguity every poet receives as his or her birthright.

As an invitation to reread Scripture, *The Scarlet Letter* directs our attention to the mystery and complexity of language more insistently than to any other matter. None of the author's pointed reflections on the moral issues the story addresses—the place of women, the problem of patriarchy and its oppressive systems, the sins of hypocrisy and self-righteousness, the abuse of power—can be adequately understood without some reckoning with the nature of words. We rely on them, even as we hedge our bets, shoring up our promises with oaths and our contracts with legalese to bung the loopholes with which they are riddled. We rely, despite considerable counterevidence, on those who weave words into laws and sermons and stories, vesting them with our hopes for the sentence that can perform the sacramental task of imparting life and grace and faith in things not seen.

But a history of abuse as old as language itself has had its two-edged effect: because people lie, some of them very persuasively, and because we are inclined to believe the lies that appeal to us most, we know we can't believe everything we hear. Because "the heart is deceitful above all things," because few, it seems "have ears to hear," and because language comes to us contaminated and culture-bound, those who seek to tell the truth are compelled to write straight with crooked lines. Emily Dickinson's imperative, "Tell all the truth but tell it slant" may also be read as a simple indicative: that is all we can do. Flannery O'Connor thinks so, anyway. Truth, she points out acerbically, generally requires distortion: "[The fiction writer's] vision is prophetic vision. . . . The prophet is a realist of distances, and it is this kind of realism that goes into great novels. It is the realism which does not hesitate to distort appearances in order to show a hidden truth."[3]

Hawthorne seems to have thought so as well. Like his fellow writers, he "lived by" words in more than one sense. His penchant for word play, his fascination with untold and untellable secrets, his suspicion of legal and theological formulae, and the narrator he invents not only to mediate the story but to editorialize on his own telling of it, bring an intensity of

---

2. Eliot, "Burnt Norton," *Four Quartets*, 19.

3. O'Connor, *Mystery and Manners*, 179.

focus almost greater than the story can bear, at times, to the language in which it is told.

Consider, for instance, how frequently the narrator pauses to call our attention to the matter of language. Repeatedly we are reminded of the evident distance between words and deeds: "Thy acts are like mercy," Hester says to Roger when he visits her in prison with soothing medications, "but thy words interpret thee as a terror!"—an observation that puts a peculiar spin on the adage that actions speak louder than words, since, as we ultimately have to acknowledge, Hester's intuition is accurate, and it is Roger's acts of mercy that belie his evil intent. Conversely, Arthur succumbs to an uncharacteristic "outbreak of temper" under Roger's hypocritical ministrations even though, he muses in bewilderment, "there had been nothing in the physician's words to excuse or palliate." We know better, since we have been made aware of a malevolent intent behind Roger's soothing rationalities that Arthur grasps only unconsciously. In both cases, the misalignment between Roger's words and his deeds troubles his hearers with an obscure foreboding.

At times words seem to take on a life of their own, independent of intention or interpretation. In her darker hours, we read, Hester "forebore to pray for enemies, lest, in spite of her forgiving aspirations, the words of blessing should stubbornly twist themselves into a curse." Arthur's words, on the other hand, seem unaccountably transformed into something like music, more evocative than indicative of meaning:

> The young pastor's voice was tremulously sweet, rich, deep, and broken. The feeling that it so evidently manifested, rather than the direct purport of the words, caused it to vibrate within all hearts, and brought the listeners into one accord of sympathy.

Indeed, the purport of his words seems on several occasions to be completely beside the point. The words of self-condemnation he utters from the pulpit, and later, dying, from the scaffold, serve ironically only to confirm his hearers' conviction of his sanctity. It is up to us, of course, to judge whether or not he has consciously calculated just such a perverse effect. The fact remains that words have effects beyond both speakers' and hearers' manifest intentions, and so must be recognized as a force, like the energies of earth, only partially subject to our understanding and control.

Nevertheless, though words transmit power, they often prove inadequate to the task of conveying the complexities of human feelings, intuitions, or needs. The "wrestle with words and meanings" becomes "intolerable" when we realize that there can be no perfect alignment between words and the felt truths grasped only in dreams or in surges of inexplicable feeling, registered not in the mind but in the body that quakes or pales or trembles for reasons that reason cannot fathom. This sad fact seems to have been a core idea for Hawthorne, whose own tragic sense of life rested largely in the paradox that, living by words, the limitations of words would mock and torment him more than most. "There can be, if I forbode aright," Arthur declares to Roger with unusual conviction, "no power, short of the Divine mercy, to disclose, whether by uttered words, or by type or emblem, the secrets that may be buried in the human heart." If this is true, then our lives are "hidden" indeed, even from ourselves, known only to a God whose countenance is veiled, whose purposes are indirectly revealed, and whose words reach us through multiple, often mangled, translations in a much-maligned book subject to the most fatal kinds of misreadings. Even were we to confess our sins with perfect intention, Arthur's words suggest, we would not do justice to the truth of the matter; our circumstances and stories, the mitigating and complicating factors that shape and determine the simplest human act, cannot be fully narrated.

So the business of telling the truth is, in a sense, doomed to incompletion. Yet story making is so fundamental to human consciousness and community, it seems as necessary as food, clothing, and shelter to sustaining life. Arthur's tragedy, Hester's sorrow, and Roger's fatal mistake lie in the secrets locked in their hearts not only out of simple willfulness, but also because their stories cannot be told in terms that would do them justice. So Arthur is right to rely on "Divine mercy"—on a God who hears and parses human speech, broken since Babel, and perfects it in a generous act of re-membering.

Even little Pearl, or perhaps especially she, feels the pain of inadequate language: what she knows she cannot tell. She resorts to symbolic fancies to speak truths the catechism makes no room for; she "sobs out her love for her mother in broken words" when her little rages are exhausted, "mumbles" into the minister's ear "such gibberish" as children are wont to invent, and acts out her wordless intuitions by pelting her mother's scarlet letter with flowers, shaking her little hand "with a variety of threatening gestures" at the mockeries of other children, taking the minister's hand, running away from her mother's voice to follow the sunshine or play with her shadow. Her solace seems mostly to inhere in an enforced but also privileged intimacy with the natural world. Among the wordless trees and by the brook whose babbling keeps her company, she finds her community and even a kind of communion that is "kind, quiet, soothing, but melancholy."

Both the solace and the melancholy associated with the natural world seem to be a function of its wordlessness. What if, in fact, they have languages of their own, inaccessible to human understanding, we are led to wonder. What if, in fact, every tree is an utterance—an idea that has biblical roots in Genesis and the Psalms—and the movement of the waves a conversation from which we are excluded? These Romantic fancies, in which Hawthorne indulged more than half seriously along with a good many of his contemporaries, are not entirely divorced from scientific efforts to map and decode the behaviors of other sentient beings and to fathom how they live and move. Such ideas about alternative forms of communication radically modify not only the sense of human "dominion" that so easily verges into hubris, but the notion that human language is God's language. If it is not, then how do we develop ears that hear "what the Spirit says"?

In the introductory "Custom House" chapter, speaking in a quasi-autobiographical voice, Hawthorne mentions seasons of torpidity and melancholy in which even nature lost its "invigorating charm" and life-giving freshness. Allusion to this loss suggests, however, that his more accustomed relationship to the natural world was one of deep receptivity to its mysteries, and to the notion that, properly "read," nature might be a vehicle of revelation and a source of sympathy. The latter idea comes up explicitly and repeatedly in the ensuing story, as in the opening chapter where the narrator points to the wild rose by the prison house door as a possible "token that the deep heart of Nature could pity and be kind to him." Roger Chillingworth's herbal pharmacopoeia are pointed out as "Nature's boon to the untutored savage," and the little brook that runs by Hester and Arthur's rock in the woods "might be traced by its merry gleam afar into the wood's heart of mystery, which had become" thanks to their brief, passionate reunion "a mystery of joy." Elsewhere shafts of sunlight seem to summon Pearl to play. Is all this simple projection? Or is "Nature" actually communicative?

The answer may lie partly in one of Hawthorne's favorite descriptive words, a sense of whose richness he shared with Thoreau, Whitman,

Melville, and Muir. The "wild" represented a quality of freedom, openness to possibility, capacity for surprise, and resiliency that all of nature seemed to partake of, including humankind at its best and most childlike. The "stern old wilderness," it would seem, is our teacher, offering a reliable corrective to the prejudices of human institutions, the excesses of human greed, and the narrowness of human imagination. We are, we might learn, too easily domesticated, and too readily seduced by the devices and desires of human minds, too easily alienated from our animal selves. The "wild, heathen nature of the forest, never subjugated by human law, nor illumined by higher truth" appears to be not only "stern," but also, and often, "sympathetic." It meets us at the level of feeling, inviting and inciting a kind of intelligence often dismissed or overlooked in human transactions. To those, like Roger, who take the time to learn its secrets, Nature is generous in disclosure. "I have learned many new secrets in the wilderness," he reports, by way of assuring Hester that his medicines are trustworthy. In Pearl's "wild" eyes lies a quality of truth as yet unconstrained and uncontaminated by social prejudice and expedient courtesies. In this word, "wild," lies a whole project of reclamation and resistance—even a theological commitment to the notion that the created order is the Creator's word to creatures—a word we do, most literally, live by.

But this idea—that the natural world is a decipherable language with a life-giving and reliable message, could we but learn to read it—offers only partial consolation for the loss of connection to an *Ursprache* or original language that was once—say, before Babel—presumably, intact, universal, precise, and adequate. Moving in Emerson's circles, Hawthorne had considerable exposure to this philological fantasy, which was one expression of the "infinite longing" that became a defining feature of Romantic thought, whose long legacy still lingers in lines like W. S. Merwin's: "I want to tell you what the forests were like / I will have to speak in a forgotten language."[4]

In its light, the history of language takes on a tragic cast, as though the acquisition of language represents a reenactment of the Fall, shattering some original experience of wholeness into word fragments we spend the rest of our lives piecing together into sentences that circle around a pregnant silence that will never, at least in this life, bring forth whole and living what it harbors.

---

4. Merwin, *The Rain in the Trees*, 65.

According to this mythic view of language, individuals as well as whole cultures experience this loss as they grow into the discourses of their communities, accommodating their healthy, malleable baby minds to the terms provided in the categories and catechisms available, naming and narrativizing their experience accordingly. "How soon," our narrator observes with what seems a note of lament, "—with what strange rapidity, indeed did Pearl arrive at an age that was capable of social intercourse beyond the mother's ever-ready smile and nonsense-words!" Pearl's early command of language seems, though, ever to lag behind the prodigious intuitions that link her as critic, spy, judge, and victim of the secretive adults she relies on. It also complicates, often painfully, her relationship with a mother whose "ready smile" tightens into frowns of anxiety as she fields Pearl's inconvenient questions and untimely moments of awkward truth telling. How much truth to tell a child and in what terms is a question every parent has to face, and most come to moments of realizing how much of conversation with children involves tricky translation issues it is tempting to resolve by postponing promises that they "will understand when they are older." But children know evasion when they see it—certainly Pearl does—and are not easily satisfied with words that mask or twist the truths they intuit.

Because the mother cannot find ways to tell her daughter a truth whole enough to honor the paradoxes she lives with, Pearl's insistent questions drive Hester deeper into the great interior silence the narrator calls a "moral wilderness." Wanting to "train up her child in the way she should go," she teaches Pearl a faith language and an ethic that exclude and condemn her, and wears the "ignominious" letter at Pearl's insistence long after she would have been permitted by others to lay it aside. Longing for something that goes beyond even Arthur's love, she lingers in the town and at the doors of the church, foregoing conversation and situating herself where she can hear only the cadences of a sermon whose words no longer seem either accessible or necessary to her. Meeting townspeople in the street, "she never raised her head to receive their greeting. If they were resolute to accost her, she laid her finger on the scarlet letter, and passed on." She was "little accustomed, in her long seclusion from society, to measure her ideas of right and wrong by any standard external to herself" and increasingly "wild" in her own thoughts which submitted less and less easily to the terms of public discourse. Her silence seems not only a retreat from community but a retreat from language itself, shaped and limited by the stringencies of Puritan patriarchy.

And yet, "The letter was the symbol of her calling." This simple sentence could well be seen as the central idea of a story that is not only a tale of a few human beings' "frailty and sorrow," or of a cultural moment fraught with its tragic drama of crime and punishment, but also an autobiographical disclosure of a man of words who is also a man of sorrows, knowing as he does how all stories end with an implicit acknowledgement that "the rest is silence." We tell what we can, and then stop at the threshold of mystery. At that point we resort to theology or music or wordless attentiveness to the subtle, wild energies that play out their quiet messages on Aeolean harps. As Hester was bound by the letter of the law, her author was bound to the law of the letter: crafting sentences that would bear the torque and weight of the unspoken, leaning into implication, inviting readers to infer, interpret, intuit, appropriate, and apply what they could, he seemed to work like the builders of dikes, making his story a stay against the confusions of history and law and theology with their extravagant and exclusionary claims that seemed to fall so far short of accounting for the truths of "the human heart."

In his own way, Hawthorne might have reiterated the cry of an ancient rabbi reading Torah: "These words are my very life!" Yet well he knew that even the words of the most life-giving sacred texts could be turned from nourishment to poison, contaminated in the act of interpretation, sometimes beyond antidote. His own stories, "Rappaccini's Daughter" and "The Birthmark," offer analogues and examples: in both, mad male scientists, Faustian seekers after heartless knowledge, poison the women they love with potions they believe will preserve and perfect the victims' lives. The tragedy of misinterpretation and misapplication of sacred words—or of any words—can be just as death-dealing.

"The letter killeth," Paul writes, "but the Spirit giveth life" (2 Cor 3:6). What, then, are men and women of letters to do with the letter? They wield an instrument that may be alternately, and sometimes simultaneously, life-giving and death-dealing. They depend upon the discernment of readers whose task it must be to complete in the labyrinthine privacies of their own culture-bound imaginations the work the writer has begun. There is no foolproof way to link words to meanings but in the living, collaborative dialogue between writer and reader. Perhaps there is always a third party to that dialogue, the Spirit that "giveth life," informing the imagination, awakening associations, offering sudden insights that come unbidden even to the most resistant or rule-bound readers. Certainly that has been the hope of those who have translated and put into public hands sacred texts whose gaps and crannies and variations and antique constructions are almost certain to baffle the unschooled reader and to feed the projections of predatory readers hunting for proof-texts. It may also at least implicitly be the hope of the writer who binds his manuscript and sends it into the world knowing its utter vulnerability to the distortions of literalistic, unimaginative, indifferent, pedantic, or one-dimensional readings. Some, perhaps for that reason, advise the young not to write "unless you must." If you must, then the letter is a symbol of your calling, too.

Many of the townspeople who came to value Hester's generous, quiet presence over the years of her solitary life among them "refused to interpret the scarlet A by its original signification." They said it meant "Able" (or "Abel," in one version), "so strong was Hester with a woman's strength." Bringing subsequent experience to bear upon the time-worn inscription, they exercised the dangerous authority inherent in public opinion to reframe and reinterpret and even reinvent history to bring it into alignment with their own lived experience of what matters and what is true. This shift suggests that to read is to enter into a precarious social contract where change may occur on both sides. Each new reading of Shakespeare or of a parable or a poem reaffirms the disturbing truth that "the past keeps changing." "Do not call it fixity," Eliot warns, "where past and future are gathered," because, he explains, "there is only the dance."[5]

Eliot's words in his last great poem echo a feeling and conviction that pervade Hawthorne's best work. We live and move and find our meanings, they both insist, in a fluid medium. Words are no more fixed than the molecules that whirl and join into temporary solidities we call nouns. They serve us as they can, linking us to one another in a "mystical body" or in the "body electric," each a locus of energy and a place where meaning may pool and gather and reflect the light. We receive them as a gift that distinguishes us from other creatures and empowers us to organize our efforts and join our lives and grieve our losses.

Writing about Dimmesdale's predecessors in the "sacred office" he occupied, Hawthorne's narrator reflects on the legacy of scholarship, shrewd minds, and "granite understanding" they left. "All that they lacked," he concludes,

---

5. Eliot, "Burnt Norton," in *Four Quartets*, 15.

was, the gift that descended upon the chosen disciples at Pentecost, in tongues of flame; symbolising, it would seem, not the power of speech in foreign and unknown languages, but that of addressing the whole human brotherhood in the heart's native language. These fathers, otherwise so apostolic, lacked Heaven's last and rarest attestation of their office, the Tongue of Flame. They would have vainly sought—had they ever dreamed of Seeking—to express the highest truths through the humblest medium of familiar words and images. Their voices came down, afar and indistinctly, from the upper heights where they habitually dwelt.

Scholarship, erudition, even the ambition that goes by the name of zeal may not, in other words, bring us closer to certain core truths that must be conveyed either by the evocative simplicity of the parables or the Beatitudes or by the tongue of flame that rises here and there out of the embers of inherited prayers in the mouths of those whose only preparation has been fidelity to what love has called them to. Arthur's troubled astonishment at the effect of his own words suggests that even those over whom that flame hovers may have no accurate sense of how they are being used. Ruefully, he asks Hester in their one private colloquy among the trees, those great keepers of secrets,

> Canst thou deem it, Hester, a consolation that I must stand up in my pulpit, and meet so many eyes turned upward to my face, as if the light of heaven were beaming from it!—must see my flock hungry for the truth, and listening to my words as if a tongue of Pentecost were speaking!—and then look inward, and discern the black reality of what they idolise? I have laughed, in bitterness and agony of heart, at the contrast between what I seem and what I am!

Arthur's agonized assessment of his own unworthiness echoes those of many saints and spiritual leaders whose words, despite themselves, it seems, have imparted blessing and inspired others to change their lives. Perhaps, we may speculate, Arthur's words really did bring a gift of new life to his congregation and to the town that came to love and forgive Hester and who found in his sermons a solace he could not himself enjoy. Perhaps words do their work in spite of the one who utters or inscribes them. Though they come to us from contaminated sources, tainted and tarnished by centuries of use and abuse, they may still carry some vestige, like the DNA in a fossil, of "original energy" that brought them forth out of the first human mouths and held them steady on pages that stand as signposts for travelers who still need stories to see by.

-3-

Become as Little Children

Except ye be converted, and become as little children,
ye shall not enter into the kingdom of heaven.

MATTHEW 18:3

"THE LITTLE BAGGAGE HATH witchcraft in her, I profess." The Reverend Wilson's rather jaundiced view of Pearl on the occasion of her first catechism casts what our narrator might call a "lurid" light on the invitation to become "as little children." Variously described as an imp, a sprite, an elf-child, a demon offspring, an emblem of sin, wild, peculiar, and uncontrollable, she challenges every sentimentality we might be tempted to indulge in with regard to the innocence and sweetness of little children. If, indeed, we are to become like them, it behooves us to inquire further into what, exactly, that invitation might mean.

Our narrator, inclined on all matters to rather free-ranging speculation, exercises that freedom with particular relish when fixing his attention on Pearl. He leads us to wonder, for instance, how much of what manifests in children may be attributed to their parents' sins—an old idea, but one that may retain more psychological relevancy than we'd like to admit, inclined as we often are, to look from the nose rings and spiked hair of a wayward youth to the parents for an explanation. He entertains the possibility that difficult children may be demon possessed—another notion from which we may recoil, though it enjoyed considerable social currency in its time. Certainly he raises for skeptical scrutiny the Calvinist doctrine of total depravity—that human nature is basically evil, tainted by original sin, and in need, from the very outset, of redemption. He even ventures beyond various misapplications of Christian doctrine to consider the possibility that children, before they are fully indoctrinated into Christian faith and culture, may bear in their psyches the stamp of some pre-Christian, pagan, Druidic, state of nature.

Consider, he seems to enjoin us, what children are really like. Are they not a lot like Pearl? Strange as she is, anyone who has spent time among preschoolers would likely attest to the plausibility of her portrait. She asks awkward questions in public. She throws things at other children. She has tantrums, followed by inexplicable resurgences of abject affection. She will not perform on command, amuses herself with narcissistic abandon, and communes with small animals. She displays breathtaking intelligence, but in oblique and symbolic ways, devised, apparently, because adult language is either inaccessible or insufficient to her purposes. She seems, even in her worst misbehavior, to live just beyond the reach of moral reasoning. Though we might now diagnose some of her more erratic behavior with the help of psychological labels, it is hard to miss the suggestion, or to resist it, that as a small child, especially in her socially difficult circumstances, she is not to be held morally accountable.

Rather, she holds the adults around her accountable. In a moment of troubling intimacy, Hester sees her own worst self "in the small black mirror of Pearl's eye," feels indicted and mocked by Pearl's inexplicable and inappropriate laughter, and is driven in desperation to ask the question that must have occurred to most parents on occasion: "Child, what art thou?" Pearl's apparently innocuous answer lands with the psychological precision of a well-aimed arrow square on the site of Hester's deepest anxiety: "Oh, I am your little Pearl!" I am, in other words, yours in ways you may or may not want to claim. I am yours by right and by assignment. I am what you named me and called me to be. I am not only bought at great price but produced like the gem in the oyster—by an invasion of your body, and a process that you governed little more than I. Pearl is aware, as all children are, of her essential dependence on a relationship she did not choose but cannot choose against. The divine love that called her into this world is proof against even the dark closet where she is shut in her mother's moments of desperation and the wrenching neglect of a man whose "little Pearl" she knows herself also to be.

If, then, we can credit Hawthorne's portrait of Pearl with "fair authority," what may she stand to teach us about what it might mean to "become as little children"? If nothing else, she serves to complicate our understanding of the relationship Jesus so often invoked to characterize both his own and our relationship to the God who brought us into being—that of child to parent. She serves to remind us that that relationship—essential, intimate, formative, and permanent—remains radically, troublingly mysterious.

Most parents, like Hester, search for signs of themselves in their children. They bear in their bodies curious resemblances to us that show up in startling, sometimes gratifying, sometimes frightening ways. This resemblance may provide a clue to one of the rich possibilities of meaning in the biblical message about our identity: know that you are made in the image of the One who made you. You bear a divine legacy that you did nothing to earn or deserve, and can do nothing to avoid. As in your biological codes, so in the spirit that animates you, you offer a testimony to his creation to any who have eyes to see. Hawthorne's narrator mercilessly reminds us that Pearl, like every child, can be seen from two opposed vantage points: even as he calls repeated attention to her beauty—"a lovely and immortal flower"—he adds that that loveliness came "out of the rank luxuriance of a guilty passion." He spares no exuberance in describing her extraordinary appeal: "such was the splendour of Pearl's own proper beauty, shining through the gorgeous robes which might have extinguished a paler loveliness, that there was an absolute circle of radiance around her on the darksome cottage floor." Undiminished, unmodified by association with its dubious roots, her beauty seems rather to come from an untouchable source beyond outside judgment. Beauty itself is closely but ambiguously linked by imagination and theology to truth and goodness.

Morality and theology seem here to share in this ambiguity. Hester's own attempts to bring her love of Pearl and her amazement at the child's exquisite beauty and intelligence into alignment with the doctrine she has been taught that deems her an illegitimate child of sin involve her in a paradox she finds it hard to resolve:

God, as a direct consequence of the sin which man thus punished, had given her a lovely child, whose place was on that same dishonoured bosom, to connect her parent for ever with the race and descent of mortals, and to be finally a blessed soul in heaven! She knew that her deed had been evil; she could have no faith, therefore, that its result would be good. Day after day she looked fearfully into the child's expanding nature, ever dreading to detect some dark and wild peculiarity that should correspond with the guiltiness to which she owed her being. Certainly there was no physical defect. By its perfect shape, its vigour, and its natural dexterity in the use of all its untried limbs, the infant was worthy to have been brought forth in Eden: worthy to have been left there to be the plaything of the angels after the world's first parents were driven out.

The narrator spares no irony in representing Hester's efforts to validate the stringent New England Calvinism of her teachers. He leaves it to us to judge the plausibility of a doctrine that would condemn a child according to the sins of its parents. Even God, he points out, appears to take quite the opposite view, and rather, by inexplicable mercy, to reward rather than punish the wayward mother, even to the promise of paradise. We don't have to look too far for corroboration of this mercy in the Gospel story of the man blind from birth in John 9 where Jesus assures the disciples, "Neither hath this man sinned, nor his parents." In light of such evidence, Hester's doubt begins to seem downright perverse, not to mention these Puritans' punishing application of the doctrine of original sin. At least according to the severest Puritanical version of this doctrine, it would be heresy to suggest that Pearl, or any child, was "worthy to have been brought forth in Eden." It seems we are forced to choose between abstract theology and the common sense and common grace that lead us to presume and protect the innocence of small children.

That innocence, however, he is careful to distinguish from blank ignorance. Pearl's luminous intelligence challenges abstract rationality and capacity for moral reasoning as defining measures of understanding. What she knows seems on occasion to exceed what her mother or the town's authorities know, and to align her much more closely with Roger Chillingworth, whose knowledge comes from close association with native peoples and with the natural world. Both she and the old physician are open to "influences" from sources either excluded, ignored, or neutralized by the over-refined logic of systematic theologies and scholarly abstractions, and even by the bland distillations of children's horn books and catechisms. Pearl seems rather to have an "intelligence that threw its quivering sunshine over [her] tiny features"; she seems to embody and refract an unmediated energy that informs her attentions and intentions with purposes she neither can nor cares to comprehend. Her intuition—teaching that comes from within rather than without—guides her flawlessly to the source of her mother's anxieties and her father's sorrowful aspect. Both her symbolic answers to the Reverend Wilson's questions ("I was plucked from the wild rose bush by the prison door") and the insistent questions that play at the edges of her mother's untold secret ("Why dost thou wear the letter on thy bosom?" and "Why does the minister keep his hand over his heart?") betray an acuity of detection and an appetite for truth we might easily recognize in many a small child. Children know more than they can say. Therapists who watch them assign roles to dolls or puppets, caregivers who work with children in trauma, parents caught out in their own attempts to smooth over awkward realities all confirm the insights offered in Pearl's story—that even the very young have access to archetypes and ways of knowing that have their own validity and, sometimes, wisdom.

Not only Pearl's intelligence but her complexity comes into focus as our narrator launches his vigorous campaign to enfranchise the young and underestimated. "Pearl's aspect," he attests, "was imbued with a spell of infinite variety; in this one child there were many children, comprehending the full scope between the wild-flower prettiness of a peasant baby, and the pomp, in little, of an infant princess." She transcends the boundaries and confuses the defining marks of class. Her capacities and promise are of greater scope than those of the adults around her, who narrow themselves to the dimensions of social norms. Her nature moreover, "appeared to possess depth, too, as well as variety," and an internal principle that defies outward control. Hester, we are told, often "felt like one who has evoked a spirit, but, by some irregularity in the process of conjuration, has failed to win the master-word that should control this new and incomprehensible intelligence." Perhaps, we are led to reflect, controlling it should not be the point.

One mark of that intelligence that sets Pearl apart is her lawlessness: "The child could not be made amenable to rules." She resists discipline to the point (which many parents will recognize) where Hester realized "it would be labour thrown away to insist, persuade, or plead." Chillingworth, observing her, remarks, not without some satisfaction, "There is no law, nor reverence for authority, no regard for human ordinances or opinions, right or wrong, mixed up with that child's composition." The narrator, putting a somewhat more positive spin on that judgment, muses, "It was as if she had been made afresh out of new elements, and must perforce be permitted to live her own life, and be a law unto herself without her eccentricities being reckoned to her for a crime." What both of them see in her we are implicitly invited to recognize in all children: a life force, a principle of being, an unfiltered openness to the world and its possibilities, an experimental willingness to act on impulse, a bold confidence, and the "beginner's mind" spiritually inclined adults strive to retrieve. In light of these attributes, it becomes harder to reckon "reverence for authority" or "regard for human ordinances or opinions" among the habits of mind most urgently to be instilled in children.

Though Hawthorne's Romantic temperament inclined to a certain excess in its epistemology of feeling and its faith in the impulses of the "heart," it still might be said that literary Romantics in the Christian tradition sought and found a usable language for reestablishing the primacy of grace over law—a core gospel message that has needed retrieval repeatedly in the dark course of Christian history. In her unrestrained, impulsive assent to the promptings of whatever spirit moves her, Pearl bodies forth a sharp and surprising critique of the legalistic constraints of New England church and culture. She "sins boldly," but, as we see toward the end of the story, when she readily forgives her father for his much neglect, her heart is open to the least evidence of genuine love and her mind, always, to what rings true. She seems to have a built-in divining rod for truth that leads her to transgress social boundaries and violate proprieties. What is uncultivated in her remains unspoiled. Her chief virtue, indeed, seems to lie in her wildness, as her mother's lies in her capacity to survive in the "moral wilderness" to which she is driven.

These terms, "wild" and "wilderness," that recur conspicuously throughout the narrative, are laden with associations both from Scripture and from early written descriptions of the "New World." The wilderness is the place where God leads and teaches a fugitive people. Outside the oppressive structures of the Egyptian city and state, the human hierarchies, the ambitions of economically prosperous and powerful people, they are faithfully cared for by a God who meets them, day by day, with manna and water from rocks. Christian colonists in the "New World" appropriated this story to their own complex purposes, and regarded themselves, conveniently, as God's people in the wilderness. But, as Hawthorne saw it, and as our narrator wryly implies, they, like many of their ancient counterparts, became arrogant and complacent about their chosenness, and impatient to impose on "wild" places the legal and moral structures that gave them a sense of safety. Terms like "howling wilderness" with "wild and ghastly scenery," the "stern old wilderness," the "wild outskirt of the earth," or the "perilous wilderness" offer us one side of the paradox that defines the wild as life-threatening. Nevertheless, as we are compelled by Hawthorne and many of his contemporaries (most notably Thoreau) to recognize, it is also the source of primal life forces endangered by the stringencies of "civilization."

All four of the major characters in the novel are, in some sense, defined by the field of tension they occupy between Christian civilization and the "wild" lands and peoples it has encroached upon. That the European conquest was a violation, even of something sacred, was a thought scarcely to be entertained by the early settlers, eager to legitimate their "errand into the wilderness" by claiming a divine mandate to occupy the land and "improve" it. But these four, in their distinct ways, represent dimensions of a predicament Hawthorne clearly saw as both perilous and promising.

Arthur had come "from one of the great English universities, bringing all the learning of the age into our wild forest land." Effective as he is at sustaining the faith of the townspeople who are susceptible to his eloquence and feel secure in his leadership, it becomes increasingly clear as the story progresses that he is unfit for his mission. His learning does not equip him for what he encounters either in the "wildness" of Hester's passion and his own, or in the wilds of the forest where, conversely, Pearl finds herself quite at home.

Roger, also university-bred, but less driven by institutional mission, has "learned many new secrets in the wilderness" which he brings back to Boston, deciding to "pitch his tent" on "this wild outskirt of the earth." He describes himself as a wanderer; both geographically and ideologically, he stands outside the institutional orthodoxies that bound Arthur's vocation. But just as Arthur pays a price for his allegiance to church and theocratic state, Roger pays a significant price for his forfeiture of institutional allegiances. Bowing to none of its constraints, he also loses access to the correction and protection afforded by the church, and succumbs, finally, to the dark and wild influences—our narrator might call them demonic—that drive him on in his vengeful Faustian quest.

Hester's occupation of both physical and moral wilderness endangers her, as well, and, were it not for her responsibilities to Pearl, by Hester's own admission, she would very likely be "driven wild," either to suicide, or to witchcraft, or into solitary exile. Only her commitment to raise her child among her own people, despite their ostracism, keeps her treading the streets of Boston with a fidelity that earns her a dubious reputation for sanctity. That commitment becomes more puzzling as the story progresses. Thanks to our narrator, with his privileged access to the secrets of Hester's heart, we know how thin is the thread that binds her to her own people. As he points out, she seems temperamentally more fit for a place of exile in the wilderness "where the wildness of her nature might assimilate itself with a people whose customs and life were alien from the law that had condemned her." He goes on to remark, "Her intellect and heart had their home, as it were, in desert places, where she roamed as freely as the wild Indian in his woods."

But the task of domesticating that wilderness is too big for one woman alone. Hester stays on the edge of town, and her heroism is finally to stay on her own terms, which, as she gathers disciples around her in her older age, constitute a kind of new covenant that quietly challenges the badly abused covenants of church and state whose excesses she knows all too well. Her staying, as well as her returning late in her life, emerge more from her own hybrid sense of home, and what seems to be a peculiar call to inhabit and explore the moral wilderness than from a sense of duty or acquiescence to the terms of Puritan piety.

For Pearl, however, wilderness is native ground. Unlike her elders, she is not conflicted about the competing claims of town and forest. The narrator compares her to wild birds with their colorful plumage, and to other "wild things" that "recognized a kindred wilderness in the human child" and entered into relationship with her in ways apparently inaccessible to adults who, too much occupied, perhaps, with "taking dominion," have lost their sense of relatedness to these other, innocent beings:

> A pigeon, alone on a low branch, allowed Pearl to come beneath, and uttered a sound as much of greeting as alarm. A squirrel, from the lofty depths of his domestic tree, chattered either in anger or merriment—for the squirrel is such a choleric and humorous little personage, that it is hard to distinguish between his moods—so

he chattered at the child, and flung down a nut upon her head. It was a last year's nut, and already gnawed by his sharp tooth. A fox, startled from his sleep by her light footstep on the leaves, looked inquisitively at Pearl, as doubting whether it were better to steal off, or renew his nap on the same spot. A wolf, it is said—but here the tale has surely lapsed into the improbable—came up and smelt of Pearl's robe, and offered his savage head to be patted by her hand. The truth seems to be, however, that the mother-forest, and these wild things which it nourished, all recognised a kindred wilderness in the human child.

The fanciful detail in this passage likens it to a fairy-tale. Indeed, it seems infused with the wishful thinking that marks our paths to fairyland. But it serves also to raise a serious question about relationship to nature, relevant then and now to serious, practical questions about how we treat the animals we raise for food, how we protect species threatened with wanton extinction, how we guard their habitats from devastation. The loss of that sense of relationship, which seems in this story relegated to the realm of children, carries, as Hawthorne, Thoreau, and others of their circle recognized, large and lasting consequences.

Pearl also identifies herself with plant life, asserting that she has been plucked off the wild rose-bush by the prison door. Her mother is not amused. Searching the child's "wild, bright, deeply black eyes," she dreads to find a "dark and wild peculiarity" that signifies some spiritual deformity produced by her mother's guilt, but also sees a reflection of her own wild fancies in Pearl's "wild energies." The word comes up so frequently as a descriptor for Pearl, it works almost as an epithet. In this wild child we are led to invest a certain hope for a new generation, able to accommodate to a new time in a new land on new terms. Unbound by what binds her elders and uncrippled by culturally constructed fears, she is equipped for exploration, and for the rise of womankind to a new relationship with man and nature, and even with the native peoples her forebears regard as "savages." As she prances about the streets of the town on election day, Pearl "ran and looked the wild Indian in the face, and he grew conscious of a nature wilder than his own." In her wildness, she is all potential—open and free and able to accommodate to the complex task of making a life in an environment that will never replicate Europe. That she finally returns to Europe, and appears to have married European nobility, is another of the many ironic turns the story takes: it is left to us to determine whether that represents a victory over circumstances, or a sad defeat of a certain hope Pearl represented whose time had not yet come.

As a lawless and wild child, though, Pearl manifests two characteristics that bear upon that hope in ways pertinent to Hawthorne's purposes as he holds her up for emulation: her anger and her laughter. Both appear at strange times and seem strangely inappropriate. In response to her mother's tears Pearl "would frown, and clench her little fist, and harden her small features into a stern, unsympathising look of discontent." Taken to the governor's house, where her mother attempts to quiet her into seemly comportment, Pearl, "in utter scorn of her mother's attempt to quiet her, gave an eldritch scream, and then became silent, not from any notion of obedience, but because the quick and mobile curiosity of her disposition was excited by the appearance of those new personages." Some of her outbursts are more explicable. Targeted by the Puritan children (whom our acerbic narrator describes with more than his usual irony), she defends herself with a fury we are encouraged to find quite understandable:

> She saw the children of the settlement on the grassy margin of the street, or at the domestic thresholds, disporting themselves in such grim fashions as the Puritanic nurture would permit; playing at going to church, perchance, or at scourging Quakers; or taking scalps in a sham fight with the Indians, or scaring one another with freaks of imitative witchcraft. Pearl saw, and gazed intently, but never sought to make acquaintance. If spoken to, she would not speak again. If the children gathered about her, as they sometimes did, Pearl would grow positively terrible in her puny wrath, snatching up stones to fling at them, with shrill, incoherent exclamations, that made her mother tremble, because they had so much the sound of a witch's anathemas in some unknown tongue.

Surely, we see, there is ample justification for her fury, and even wisdom in her reticence to engage with these violent offspring upon whom, we infer, the rod has not been spared. What Pearl comes to hate seems worthy of honest hatred:

> The truth was, that the little Puritans, being of the most intolerant brood that ever lived, had got a vague idea of something outlandish, unearthly, or at variance with ordinary fashions, in the mother and child, and therefore scorned them in their hearts, and not unfrequently reviled them with their tongues. Pearl felt the

> sentiment, and requited it with the bitterest hatred that can be sup-
> posed to rankle in a childish bosom.

Her hatred comes forth in screams and shouts, uttered with "a terrific volume of sound, which, doubtless, caused the hearts of the fugitives to quake within them." Once expended, she is satisfied, returns quietly to her mother and "look[s] up, smiling, into her face. All children seem capable of just such instant transformations as this: fully in the moment, their peace, like their fury, comes to them whole and unstinting.

We may sympathize with the child's pain at exclusion and judgment as well as her recoil from play that replicates religious excesses. We may even credit her with righteous indignation. But the fact remains that Pearl is not a nice girl. Her "caprice," her evident indifference to her mother's sorrows, her aggressive interrogations of the suffering minister mark her as an antagonist even to those who are gentlest toward her. She seems happiest out of human company. If therein she again accurately represents what "little children" are like, her behavior must surely give us pause before we consent to hold it as a standard.

And it should. But Pearl's anger raises a key question for morally sensitive readers: how do we measure the virtues of obedience, gentleness, and submissiveness against the sometimes necessary fury evoked by injustice or violence or prejudice? Religious legitimations for exploitation, injustice and even genocide we have always with us. Polite agreement to accept even the most consequential political differences, the self-protective strategies of bland conformity or retreat behind abstract principles that support the status quo have historically made way for atrocities utterly incompatible with the way of a peacemaking Christ. Pearl's anger is exactly the kind of indictment that is urgent and necessary in times when abuse of power has become normative.

When anger doesn't serve, there is laughter. As Luther put it, reminding us of the power of laughter in the face of abuses of power, "The devil cannot bear to be mocked." Pearl's laughter, like her anger, is aimed with eerie aptitude at any who seek to control her on false pretexts. She mocks pretense with a freedom that is truly frightening to those heavily invested in a social politics of control, giving them "a bright, but naughty smile of mirth and intelligence" that escalates more than once into raucous laughter. Typically, the narrator teases us into associating her weird laughter with that of witches, fiends, and other beings.

Pelting her mother with flowers, aimed skillfully at the letter on her breast, Pearl is amused despite the evident pain this gentle battery inflicts: "At last, her shot being all expended, the child stood still and gazed at Hester, with that little laughing image of a fiend peeping out—or, whether it peeped or no, her mother so imagined it—from the unsearchable abyss of her black eyes." One wonders at this laughter: is it mockery? Is it simply childlike amusement at a spontaneous game of skill, bearing no reference to the potent symbolism of the act? Or is it perhaps an invitation to receive the battery of flowers as an antidote to the scorn and "ignominy" that has been aimed at her by so many others? This last reading would suggest not only wisdom, but tenderness in Pearl's odd laughter, and would attribute Hester's darker reading to her own inability to receive her child's play as an act of grace. Similarly, when Hester is driven to tears of frustration or bewilderment (another frequent and pregnant descriptor for her chronic state of mind) Pearl's response is often first anger, then the weird laughter that seems to demand some otherworldly explanation: "Not seldom she would laugh anew, and louder than before, like a thing incapable and unintelligent of human sorrow." Cruel as it may seem, the very strangeness of this response invites further speculation: could it be that this laughter betokens not incomprehension, but a wider comprehension of the human story that ends in a promise of life beyond tears? Perhaps—we are at least invited to consider—this child's perspective is aligned with a truth much larger than that of adults enmeshed in their personal stories of shame and guilt and pain.

Pearl's laughter is not, in any case, only strange or mocking, but "full of merriment and music." Like her dancing step and her propensity to "chase the sunshine," she seems to have an innate gift for happiness that transcends the bleak circumstances of her lonely life and is nourished by nature itself. It was something of a Romantic commonplace in mid-nineteenth-century writing, to personify the natural world, to attribute feeling and intention to natural forces and to assign to "the deep heart of nature" a godlike, if morally neutral, role in human fate. Hawthorne's appropriation of that convention is infused with and enriched by a theological sensibility that, if not systematically worked out, nevertheless points us repeatedly back to the Scriptures that, he seemed to believe, needed and deserved radical rereading.

And this is one of those scriptural words, compelling and mysterious and pregnant with possibility: "Except ye be converted, and become as little children, ye shall not enter into the kingdom of heaven." To read Pearl's story as a parable is to see it as a teaching about respecting the complexity as well as the innocence of children: children know more than they can say. The Spirit dances and prays within them. They are fully capable vehicles of grace and truth. Not having learned the skills and strategies of self-deception, they are quick to recognize and reject falsehood. They do not belong to their parents, but to God and to the natural realm: they are wise as animals are wise in choosing life and survival by whatever means present themselves. They live in the moment, and respond with their whole hearts. They are often surprisingly open-hearted and quick to forgive.

This last attribute is beautifully attested to in the final chapters of the story. As Arthur stands dying on the scaffold where Hester was condemned, he summons the child as "my little Pearl," and she comes to him, after years of neglect and betrayal, not reluctantly, but "with the bird-like motion, which was one of her characteristics," she "flew to him, and clasped her arms about his knees." And following his impassioned but strangely ambiguous confession, unimpeded by Hester's reticence or Roger's animosity, Pearl accepts Arthur's second invitation without hesitation and kisses him on the lips there in the public square. Thereupon,

> A spell was broken. The great scene of grief, in which the wild infant bore a part had developed all her sympathies; and as her tears fell upon her father's cheek, they were the pledge that she would grow up amid human joy and sorrow, nor forever do battle with the world, but be a woman in it. Towards her mother, too, Pearl's errand as a messenger of anguish was fulfilled.

This remarkable, and beautifully tender passage marks the child's passage into the adult world, equipped as she needs to be by this occasion of forgiveness and released by the completion of a task specific to childhood. It may be, if we read the psychological literature rightly, that all children have to forgive their parents in order to emerge whole of heart into their own adult lives. Some, of course, never accomplish this. But what Hawthorne calls our attention to in Pearl's story is that forgiveness, one of the greatest and hardest virtues, is an essentially childlike act. Children accept life as it comes to them, and adapt. They are not yet caught in the web of time and storied identity that might entangle them in the past.

Still, they have their own purposes, and serve them the better for not "taking thought." Pearl's "errand" to her mother is not unlike other children's, exceptional as her circumstances are. Whether they delight or break their parents' hearts, children are occasions of costly learning. As such they serve purposes beyond what they may imagine. Only when they arrive at a mature sense of their own intentions do their hearts begin to become, as Jeremiah believed, "deceitful above all things, and desperately wicked." Though, as Pearl notices, the sunshine "does not love" her mother, she offers confidently to "run and catch it." "I am but a child," she explains. "It will not flee from me—for I wear nothing on my bosom yet!"

Bleak as it may be about the prospects of surviving spiritually intact into adulthood, at least in a culture governed by narrow theocrats and power derived from white male privilege, Pearl's story ends on a note of hope for children of single parents, children who are ostracized, isolated, poorly socialized, untrained. There is, this story insists, a divinity that shapes their ends, roughhew them how we will. They are more capable, resilient, adaptive, crafty, and spiritually aware than we may imagine. And if, like Pearl, they are loved, even by one anxious, depressed, uncertain, poor and marginalized parent, that love can suffice.

-4-

Render Unto Caesar

*Render therefore unto Caesar the things which are Caesar's
and unto God the things that are God's.*

MATTHEW 22:21

WE KNOW THE STORY: Pharisees, seeking to trick Jesus, ask him whether they should pay taxes to the occupying Roman government. If he says yes, they can identify him as a despicable collaborator and rally the oppressed Jewish community against him. If he says no, he puts himself in legal jeopardy as a tax resister. The riddle he gives them for an answer leaves us all with a Möbius strip of moral reasoning that remains a challenge to all who claim allegiance to both God and the state: "Whose is this image and superscription?" It is, of course, Caesar's. "Render therefore unto Caesar what is Caesar's, and unto God what is God's." Though at face value the response might seem to suggest that one pay one's taxes, the spin on this answer forestalls such a simple conclusion. Above the image of Caesar on the denarius Jesus holds up for examination are inscribed words that proclaim that Caesar is god. So unless one wants to underwrite that presumption, the question of what one owes the state remains uncomfortably open: What *is* Caesar's? And what *is* God's? What

59

are the claims of the state upon its citizens, and what are the limits of those claims? And by what criteria do we decide?

In *Under God* Garry Wills comments astutely upon Americans' confused legacy of civil religion rooted in colonial theocracy and complicated by a theory of manifest destiny that masked generations of greed and ambition with the cloak of divine right.[1] The confusion about what is God's and what is Caesar's outlasted the explicitly religious compacts and covenants of early New England into a nineteenth-century culture in which evangelical Protestantism became "the dominant force in American life" and the "unofficial religious establishment" of American politics.[2] As the American empire has expanded to cover the globe with corporate capitalism, legislators and heads of state have continued to invoke sometimes vague, sometimes explicit religious justifications for expansions and abuses of power. Even as Hawthorne wrote in 1850, human rights and property rights of slaves and native peoples continued to be systematically violated. So, too, as he clearly recognized, were the basic rights of women, who remained disenfranchised by law and custom.

In the wake of Andrew Jackson's genocidal policies and in the midst of bitter debates about slavery, the question what is God's and what is Caesar's had acquired new dimensions of meaning. John Brown's martyrdom, Thoreau's tax resistance, Henry Ward Beecher's abolitionist sermons and Frederick Douglass's shocking personal narrative put the question to Hawthorne's generation as it had never quite been put before. So, in *The Scarlet Letter* Hawthorne takes it up with characteristic penetrating indirection, leading readers to reconsider the role of government and the rights of individuals in the most poignant case possible: a dispute over the right of a parent to keep her child.

The question arises in chapters 7 and 8 when Hester takes Pearl to the governor's mansion. Her mission is to defend her right to keep the child. People in the town, Governor Bellingham among them, have developed a plan to transfer Pearl to "wiser and better guardianship than Hester Prynne's." In that epoch, our enigmatic narrator recalls (in words cited heretofore),

> matters of even slighter public interest, and of far less intrinsic weight than the welfare of Hester and her child, were strangely mixed up with the deliberations of legislators and acts of state. The

1. Wills, *Under God*.

2. Marsden, *Fundamentalism and American Culture*, 6, quoted in Wills, 19.

period was hardly, if at all, earlier than that of our story, when a
dispute concerning the right of property in a pig not only caused
a fierce and bitter contest in the legislative body of the colony, but
resulted in an important modification of the framework itself of
the legislature.

The odious comparison presses the point: what is the government's business and by what right does it regulate individuals' claims to children
or chattel? Moreover, when the government presumes to regulate lives
and property beyond where it is necessary to keep the peace, it appears
that its interference works to weaken and confuse its original purposes
and squander its energies. The more consequential question here, however, concerns not property disputes, but basic God-given rights. If they
are indeed God-given, as the Declaration of Independence affirms, they
would seem to lie beyond the jurisdiction of the state, except in cases of
obvious neglect or mistreatment.

The question whether and under what circumstances the government may take children away from their birth parents remains a matter of
legal dispute. We rightly set a high premium on the claims of even mani-
festly negligent or abusive parents. And the old American debate about
the extent of government jurisdiction in citizens' private lives intensifies
when the sanctity of family—even broken families—is threatened.

Hester's twofold defense against Governor Bellingham's carefully
framed threat to take Pearl away from her "for [the] little one's temporal and eternal welfare" deserves some consideration. First, she insists,
"laying her finger on the red token" she has been forced to wear, "I can
teach my little Pearl what I have learned from this!" Ironically, her fitness
as a mother may well lie in the fruits of her crime and punishment, her
public shame, the self-reflection, and indeed the theological and political
reflection, it has occasioned. What she has learned from it is detailed with
sobering clarity in chapter 13, "Another Look at Hester." She has learned
humility in unrequited and often unappreciated service. She has learned
how to survive by her own labor. She has learned empathy with those
who suffer—not the condescension that offers token comfort for its own
gratification, but fellow feeling that can only come from deep recognition
of shared vulnerability. She has learned to look death in the face and to
accept life on its harsh terms. She has learned to be both submissive and
subversive, keeping her own counsel until forced, as on this occasion, to
speak on her own behalf. What she has to teach Pearl is a complex lesson:

your rights as a citizen are abridged by your sex. Your relationship to God and God's creation is mediated by church and state powers that deny mystery for the sake of control. Truth is more complicated than what you have learned in your catechism: those who standardize it and apply it rigidly betray it. If you are to live truly, you must be wily as well as wise. Hester has acquired what we might today call "street" wisdom. She has paid for understanding with rejection, and so learned what can be learned only from the margins.

Hester's second line of defense, her first having failed to persuade, is to turn to Arthur, appointing him her advocate with the full force of suppressed passion as well as a moral authority no one recognizes more clearly than he:

> "God gave her into my keeping!" repeated Hester Prynne, raising her voice almost to a shriek. "I will not give her up!" And here by a sudden impulse, she turned to the young clergyman, Mr. Dimmesdale, at whom, up to this moment, she had seemed hardly so much as once to direct her eyes. "Speak thou for me!" cried she. "Thou wast my pastor, and hadst charge of my soul, and knowest me better than these men can. I will not lose the child! Speak for me! Thou knowest—for thou hast sympathies which these men lack—thou knowest what is in my heart, and what are a mother's rights, and how much the stronger they are when that mother has but her child and the scarlet letter! Look thou to it! I will not lose the child! Look to it!"

The dramatic irony of her appeal, freighted with their undisclosed secret, does not diminish its force and poignancy as a cry that might echo in that of many an unwed mother looking to the state for justice, to men for support, and to God, who knows the heart's darkest secrets and forgives them, for vindication. That a child is a gift from God often bestowed on parents ill equipped for childcare is perfectly evident to any believer. No Puritan cleric would have disputed the basic truth of her argument, though they might find others to justify Pearl's removal. But here the elders' ecclesiastical reasoning tends toward a common good defined less generously than that of the liberal and even extravagant God manifested in the mysteries of "Nature" to which Hawthorne so consistently directs our attention. What institutional hierarchies protect, he implies, tends often to be their own perpetuity and power rather than the unique, varied, imperfect, suffering lives of their members.

Hester's specific appeal to Arthur involves him, of course, not only as pastor, but as a party more interested in Pearl's fate than anyone else suspects (except we privileged lot who enjoy the benefit of the narrator's broad hints). Still, it is as pastor that she invokes his help—a fact that raises pertinent questions about what might be the duties of a caring pastor toward the outlaws, suspects, convicts, and disturbers of the (sometimes spurious) peace. As her pastor, he has "charge" of her soul, or so they both believe. Under the rubric of Puritan law and custom, it was his business to discern what served her and Pearl's spiritual welfare, to define that welfare according to a thoroughly informed reading of Scripture, and to accompany his application of scriptural principles with prayerful pastoral attention to their needs. All those high duties, however, as our narrator makes painfully clear, are imbedded in a culture that has largely succeeded in making the church a collaborator in a statutory order mostly advantageous to those in power. Underwritten by the elaborate semiotics of architecture, costume, symbols of power, and public ritual, even the most conscientious of pastors (and surely Arthur was one such—or so we are intermittently encouraged to believe) must find himself in a golden trap where complicity is the price of his access to the pulpit.

Arthur's election-day sermon offers a case in point. "In compliance with a custom thus easily established and ever since observed," he is to preach a sermon on the occasion of the new governor's election to office. Whether this gesture signifies the church's blessing upon the state or vice versa, it certainly aligns them in an enterprise whose deepest purposes we are led to question. Can there be integrity, the narrator seems to wonder, where church and state have become necessary to each other's proper function? Would it not better insure accountability in both if they performed reciprocally as check and balance? The complicity of the two seats of power is manifest on the election day in question by the highly symbolic procession of "worthies" through the town, toward the church door, open, it seems, to all but Hester and her ilk. "First came the music," we read, which, though imperfectly performed, achieved the object for which it was intended, "that of imparting a higher and more heroic air" to the procession of powerful men whose slow progress it heralded. At this point we might briefly pause to recognize how music has undergirded and motivated the wide spectrum of human enterprise from praising God "with lyre and harp" to sounding the martial drumbeats that lead soldiers to kill. "Imparts" is the operative verb in this sentence. The music some still believed originated in the vibrations of the heavenly "spheres" has been domesticated to an instrument of civil authority.

Thus, after the musicians come the soldiers, who, having "felt the stirrings of martial impulse," were engaged in learning "the practices of war." Elevation of warfare as a necessary function of both church and state was hardly peculiar either to the theocracy here painted in such vivid symbolic terms, or to Hawthorne's antebellum generation, preparing itself for the "great battlefields" of the costliest war in American history up to its time. The "brilliancy of effect" our narrator pauses to note, achieved not only by fanfare, but by feathers and burnished steel, seems utterly to obscure the muddy realities of warfare.

In the wake of these living images of various forms of worldly power come the "men of civil eminence," trumping the "vulgar" soldiers' march with what our narrator identifies as a "stamp of majesty"—a phrase rendered more than a little ironic by the reminder that these English settlers had left "king, nobles, and all degrees of awful rank behind." These vestiges of monarchy are ambiguous at best. "The people," he muses, "possessed by hereditary right the quality of reverence, which, in their descendants, if it survive at all, exists in smaller proportion, and with a vastly diminished force in the selection and estimate of public men. The change may be for good or ill, and is partly, perhaps, for both."

Something, no doubt, is lost in the forfeiture of court and king as living embodiments of divine right and rule. But in an American setting the hypocrisies endemic to such displays appear especially painfully evident. They seem, we are told, every bit the counterparts of the House of Peers or the Privy Council of the Sovereign—no different, that is, from those against whom they so righteously rebelled. The "primitive statesmen" the narrator names—Bradstreet, Endicott, Dudley, and Bellingham (all of whom were actual civil leaders of the Puritan settlers, and at least one of whom was associated with an unorthodox marriage that caused local scandal)[3]—"seem to have been not often brilliant, but distinguished by a ponderous sobriety, rather than activity of intellect." One wonders at this backhanded compliment, whether that sobriety might not have been bought at a fatal price. They were men who "stood up for the welfare of the state like a line of cliffs against a tempestuous tide." But by now, having

3. Online: http://www.olgp.net/chs/d1/bellingham.htm. For an interesting note on Richard Bellingham's controversial marriage see Goss, "About Richard Bellingham."

been schooled in skepticism for the twenty-one subversive chapters preceding this scene, we know enough to question the wry metaphor: cliffs against the tide slowly erode. They rely entirely on mass and density to maintain their integrity, but their devolution is inevitable.

Moreover, the narrator suggests, their mass and density may be merely a function of circumstance. Under other conditions, these men might be readily recognizable as compatriots to the pirates and outlaws they curiously tolerate:

> The buccaneer on the wave might relinquish his calling and become at once if he chose, a man of probity and piety on land; nor, even in the full career of his reckless life, was he regarded as a personage with whom it was disreputable to traffic or casually associate. Thus the Puritan elders in their black cloaks, starched bands, and steeple-crowned hats, smiled not unbenignantly at the clamour and rude deportment of these jolly seafaring men.

This curious little aside emphasizes how psychologically and politically interdependent are the keepers of the law and the outlaws—the latter perhaps the shadow of the former, necessary to each other as night and day. One might think, by way of analogy, of more recent forms of corruption in high places—government and corporate leaders paying off leaders of drug cartels, supplying arms to dictators, outsourcing their own brutality. So the appearance of pirates or buccaneers appears not only acceptable but reassuring to the passing elders—perhaps as much so as the woman whose scarlet letter signifies a public inscription of their control, and who serves, like the rowdy men at the margins, as a vehicle upon which to project their own unacknowledged appetites and impulses.

Following close in the footsteps of these elders, but with less complacency, comes Arthur, the "young and eminently distinguished divine." Here, as our attention turns again to the troubled young pastor, the narrator spells out more frankly the conflicts of interest that characterized the church-state relationship and situated clerics in a field of tension:

> His was the profession at that era in which intellectual ability displayed itself far more than in political life; for—leaving a higher motive out of the question it offered inducements powerful enough in the almost worshipping respect of the community, to win the most aspiring ambition into its service. Even political power—as in the case of Increase Mather—was within the grasp of a successful priest.

The temptation to use religious authority for personal or political gain—one of the three satanic temptations Jesus underwent and resisted—could not be more explicitly acknowledged, including again, as it disturbingly does, the name of one of the most stringent and respected of the actual church leaders of the generation here reimagined. Hovering on that blurry margin between history and fiction, surmise mingles with suspicion, both of the characters whose names have entered the historical record and of those who did the recording. Characteristically, the narrator leaves it to us to judge whether Arthur has succumbed to the "inducements" he names or whether (as there is also fair authority for believing) his eloquence, dignity, and intellectual power are fruits of authentic penitence, plumbed and transformed into efficacious proclamation. Sympathetic readers may be strongly inclined to believe the latter: he is young and vigorous, unusually energized and attractive on this occasion, and "his strength seemed not of the body. It might be spiritual and imparted to him by angelical ministrations." Or perhaps it was the result of a rich period of self-reflection, or a response to the inspiring music. Yet even if all these things be true, we are reminded, no institutional power should go unquestioned. The narrator, after these speculations, delivers his own judgment that Arthur's unusual force and charisma are like the final show of life force in a dying body, a last gasp, so to speak, from one nearly spent.

And in the service of what? This seems the key question to consider in Arthur's case. Whom has he served? God or Caesar, or simply his own faltering security? The question arises in the opening scene where we are led to see him in terms of the compromises he makes to maintain his rank and authority and remains open even at the end of the story. His dying act, which at first blush appears to be a dramatic confession, actually serves further to confirm his followers in their enshrinement of him and all he stands for. The faith of his followers is reinforced, the church strangely vindicated, and his troubled conscience buried with him. He has not challenged the authority of the state. Despite the exquisite torments he suffers from a fine intellect, a sensitive heart, and a delicate conscience, he has done nothing to bring about the kind of radical change envisioned in the narrator's most candid reflections: that "As a first step, the whole system of society is to be torn down and built up anew." None of his internal anguish effects any material change in the functioning of patriarchal rule. He has not helped to empower and affirm the gifts of women for the larger community. He has not listened to the little child who offered him so many opportunities to let truth and even scandal awaken the whole town to their habitual self-deceptions. He has not restored the radical message of the Gospels or the awful mystery of Jesus' life and acts to a people living on the starvation rations of domesticated and compromised message filtered through a fine mesh of political negotiations held taut by the brokers of power.

So it seems that Arthur has given unto Caesar rather more than was Caesar's, and, insofar as he honestly mistook the mandates of the state for those of the church, and those of the church for God's own, his story may be read as a classic tragedy of misapprehension. But we are led finally to ponder more than the tragic implications either of Arthur's ambivalence or of Hester's unfulfilled promise. The question Jesus raised about what is Caesar's and what is God's comes more than once in this story to the larger, and very sharp, if implicit, point: what if everything is God's? What if the state has no legitimate role except to protect and support what "Nature" brings forth? To reframe the question this radically leads us to recognize in this story the tension between Calvinist and Anabaptist understandings of government that has divided American Christianity from the beginning. The former accents the legitimacy of civil power; the latter, its limits and inherent dangers. Thoreau's dictum, "That government is best which governs least" (immediately raised to "that government is best which governs not at all"[4]), must come to mind as we consider how Hawthorne's own association with the political skeptics, utopians, radicals and romantics of his generation is reflected and articulated in this story. Echoes of Emerson's *Nature* and Thoreau's *Walden* as well as of Beecher's radical abolitionism and Fuller's feminism all find their way into a theology of individual, mystical connection to the God of "Nature" who addresses humankind more directly and reliably in the "text" of the created order than through any human institution. And if that view of the divine governs one's reading of the Gospels, the question that emerges inevitably is what it might mean to "give God what is God's."

Hester's story offers a partial answer to that question. What she learns in her solitary years is what may perhaps be learned only when one stands a bit outside the laws and institutions that dictate social, political, and theological norms. In those years she has, as our narrator bluntly puts it, "climbed to a higher point" than the elevation of the scaffold where

4. Thoreau, *Walden and Other Writings*, 633.

she first suffered punishment. She sees from a higher place, attained after long wandering in the "dark labyrinth of mind" with "home and comfort nowhere." It is the wilderness experience that gives her the intellectual maturity and spiritual freedom necessary to a prophet, and it is as prophet that she appears in her final scene. With characteristic, but gentle, irony, the narrator confides that earlier in her life Hester had nurtured and then given up the hope that she might be a "prophetess" who could bear and impart a new vision and vigor to the relationship of "man and woman" and therein a new approach to the most fundamental questions of human community and governance. Such a prophet would serve to teach us "how sacred love should make us happy," and, we may infer, how that love might be lived out and supported by a human order more aligned with the benign forces and lessons of nature. She seems innocently, and blessedly, unaware that she has, in fact, become such a prophetic presence by the end of her life of penance, reflection, and quiet resistance:

> . . . as Hester Prynne had no selfish ends, nor lived in any measure for her own profit and enjoyment, people brought all their sorrows and perplexities, and besought her counsel, as one who had herself gone through a mighty trouble. Women, more especially— in the continually recurring trials of wounded, wasted, wronged, misplaced, or erring and sinful passion—or with the dreary burden of a heart unyielded, because unvalued and unsought came to Hester's cottage, demanding why they were so wretched, and what the remedy! Hester comforted and counselled them, as best she might. She assured them, too, of her firm belief that, at some brighter period, when the world should have grown ripe for it, in Heaven's own time, a new truth would be revealed, in order to establish the whole relation between man and woman on a surer ground of mutual happiness.

Her assurance, her belief, the comfort and counsel she is able to offer, have been distilled in a lifetime of attentiveness to the language of "the heart" so central to Hawthorne's epistemology. Revelation, in her world (and perhaps in his) is epiphanic, personal, and beyond regulation. It imparts psychological insight (sometimes unsought and unwelcome, like the shocking intuitions that leave the minister "in a maze"). It also imparts empathy, not only as a kind of emotional competence but as a source of usable wisdom. Giving God what is God's—seeking no profit in a capitalist culture, no status in a class order, no authority in a guild of men, nor even a place to "lay her head" in the shelter of the town, offering service without recognition, expending her skills without credentials or rewards, she leads those around her to a deeper level of questioning, reflection, hope, and perhaps in time, renewal. In that life of self-giving, though not without its bitterness and very human conflicts, she becomes Christ-like in conspicuous and surprising ways: she listens to inner wisdom and expends her energies selflessly on those who have little or no appreciation of who she is. The narrator's description of her return to the colony after long absence seems deliberately to link her reappearance to the stories of Jesus' reappearances among those who knew him but did not recognize his divine identity:

> one afternoon some children were at play, when they beheld a tall woman in a gray robe approach the cottage-door. In all those years it had never once been opened; but either she unlocked it or the decaying wood and iron yielded to her hand, or she glided shadow-like through these impediments—and, at all events, went in.

The suggestion of supernatural powers takes us to the outer edge of "fancy," but also points to the serious possibility that those who give God what is God's become more like God, more capable of miraculous things, and dwell in this world on new terms, under a covenant of grace barely imaginable to those who live by Caesar's laws.

-5-

Confess One to Another

Confess your faults, one to another.

JAMES 5:16

STANDING ON THE SCAFFOLD, exposed to a hostile and curious crowd, Hester Prynne keeps a silence that is more defiant than compliant. She has refused and continues to refuse to name the father of her illegitimate child. Governor Bellingham, "speaking in an authoritative voice," appeals to her pastor, the hapless Arthur, to take up the task of persuading her to confess, pointing out that he is responsible for her soul, and therefore the appropriate one to "exhort her to repentance and to confession, as a proof and consequence thereof." Oddly enough (we muse, already cleverly suspecting his conflict of interest), Arthur is loath to take on this particular task. He argues that "it were wronging the very nature of woman to force her to lay open her heart's secrets in such broad daylight, and in presence of so great a multitude." Governor Bellingham meets that empathetic (albeit self-serving) objection with one that shifts the theological ground: "Truly, as I sought to convince him, the shame lay in the commission of the sin, and not in the showing of it forth."

This polite little scuffle, performed before an audience with a whetted appetite for scandal, raises a weighty question that resurfaces repeatedly in the ensuing story: when, to whom, and on what terms is confession "meet and right" and necessary for the healing of the soul and of the community? The flip side of that question seems to have preoccupied Hawthorne in an intensely personal way: is it wise, or even possible, to tell the whole truth to those whose hearing is distorted by prejudice, fear, or simplistic presumptions? When one has good reason to believe the complexities of one's predicament will be oversimplified or entirely overlooked, how can confession serve any beneficial purpose? And how, for that matter, can the "secrets of the heart" be told adequately in a social and ecclesial discourse that privileges abstract principles over feeling, and law over love? The question indicts the bleak version of Puritan piety that Hawthorne believed continued to afflict the American church with a legacy of legalism, and leaves the more poignant open question, to whom, then, shall we unburden ourselves of the guilt that weighs on our hearts?

Everyone in this story has a secret: Hester, Arthur, and Roger, all suffer the dire consequences of undisclosed secrets, which appear to be the immediate cause of Arthur's illness, the source of Hester's soul-sapping bitterness, and in Roger (as in Mistress Hibbens) to manifest in deformities of body and character. But, as Arthur discerns in a state of telepathic mania recorded in "The Minister in a Maze," not only he and his partners in sin but every passing parishioner conceals untold secrets behind a mask of respectability. Even little Pearl, frank, direct, and sometimes harsh in her childish openness, speaks in riddles to those in authority and appears driven to a subversiveness made necessary in a climate of secrecy where truth, as she feels or fathoms it, can be told only by indirection.

Nevertheless, though confession would seem to be the appropriate resolution to these spiritual ills, it carries its own uncertain consequences, as our narrator reminds us on more than one occasion. Consider, for example, the matter of whether Arthur ought, for the sake of truth, loyalty, and love, to confess to being Hester's partner in sin. If, as most of us assume, he was Hester's lover, allowing her to suffer public punishment alone is surely a despicable act of cowardice—or so many a young reader has vehemently observed. Yet our psychologically astute narrator won't let that judgment stand without inviting us at least to consider reasons why his silence might be not only prudent but wise and even courageous.

Several factors in Arthur's case support this surprising point of view. First, it is made clear that the town not only reveres the young pastor but depends upon him for what spiritual—and, in this little theocracy, also political—stability they enjoy. A public scandal that shook their faith in him would shake their faith altogether, since he is, for them, a "type of Christ." Arthur takes this dependence seriously; it contributes to his torment as, day after day he attempts to safeguard his parishioners' peace of mind by sacrificing his own. In a cautiously theoretical argument with Roger over the value of confession, he posits the case of pastors who, knowing their own sinfulness, do not confess it publicly:

> . . . retaining, nevertheless, a zeal for God's glory and man's welfare, they shrink from displaying themselves black and filthy in the view of men; because, thenceforward, no good can be achieved by them; no evil of the past be redeemed by better service. So, to their own unutterable torment, they go about among their fellow-creatures, looking pure as new-fallen snow, while their hearts are all speckled and spotted with iniquity of which they cannot rid themselves.

The pragmatic plausibility of this argument must give us pause, especially where the pastor is not easily replaceable, and the town's spiritual welfare is, as the governor reminds him, his to oversee.

Secondly, as becomes particularly clear in Arthur's final election sermon, his solitary struggle to live with the untold secret heightens his insight into others' souls and his empathy for them in their own spiritual squalor. His secret sorrow is evidently a source of power in his preaching. His exceptional eloquence appears to be a direct result of the tension between what he knows of himself and what he makes public:

> . . . even when the minister's voice grew high and commanding—when it gushed irrepressibly upward—when it assumed its utmost breadth and power, so overfilling the church as to burst its way through the solid walls, and diffuse itself in the open air—still, if the auditor listened intently, and for the purpose, he could detect the same cry of pain. What was it? The complaint of a human heart, sorrow-laden, perchance guilty, telling its secret, whether of guilt or sorrow, to the great heart of mankind; beseeching its sympathy or forgiveness,—at every moment,—in each accent,—and never in vain! It was this profound and continual undertone that gave the clergyman his most appropriate power.

This remarkable testimony to the paradoxical transformation of Arthur's evil into good has to make us wonder whether that good has so outweighed the good of confession in this instance, that he has, in fact, chosen the better part in remaining silent. The "irrepressible" energy of the unstated seems to contribute focus and power to his preaching precisely by having been repressed. The narrator also leaves provocatively open the matter of whether Arthur's burden is actual guilt or rather sorrow—or whether his guilt has given him a greater capacity for the general sorrow that enables compassion.

Thirdly, Arthur wrestles with the cruel paradox that an act of love, especially one that produces a beautiful child, would have to be condemned and repented as unmitigatedly sinful. To confess that sin would be to deny the element of blessing in both the love and its issue. The narrator, musing on this apparent irony, states it baldly: "God, as a direct consequence of the sin which man thus punished, had given her a lovely child, whose place was on that same dishonoured bosom, to connect her parent for ever with the race and descent of mortals, and to be finally a blessed soul in heaven!" It would seem by this logic that just as all our good is tainted with sin, so our sins may be mitigated by some goodness at work wherever there is life and breath.

This ambiguity is embodied memorably in the iconic image of Hester on the scaffold as a replica of the "image of the Divine Maternity, which so many illustrious painters have vied with one another to represent." The comparison itself raises the thorny question how such beauty can co-exist with corruption. Even as he posits the quandary, the dogma he insists upon seems to belie itself: "Here, there was the taint of deepest sin in the most sacred quality of human life, working such effect, that the world was only the darker for this woman's beauty, and the more lost for the infant that she had borne." If we resist that judgment, we are left to consider what might be the moral alternatives. Are we to confess as sins those acts of our lives that, by pure grace, have been turned to a good better than we could have imagined? Pearl's very existence challenges her father's sorrow and impedes whole-hearted repentance.

Fourthly, Arthur's resistance to confession has theological as well as psychological grounding: good Protestant that he is, eschewing sacramental confession, he recognizes God's judgment seat as the only tribunal before which his sins can be justly judged. No one but God is in a position to see lives and motives with whole sight and rightly extend absolution.

In response to Roger's indirect but insistent urging that he confess for the sake of both spiritual and physical health (an argument, by the way, whose legitimacy bears acknowledgement, whatever we think of Roger's motives), Arthur argues,

> There can be, if I forbode aright, no power, short of the Divine mercy, to disclose, whether by uttered words, or by type or emblem, the secrets that may be buried in the human heart. The heart, making itself guilty of such secrets, must perforce hold them, until the day when all hidden things shall be revealed.

In Roger, whose relentless predatory pursuit of Arthur's secret is fast reaching a climax at this point, Arthur seems to recognize (or, as he more pertinently puts it, "forbode") the danger of confessing to one who would abuse his confidence. Roger's argument, though made vivid in the fanciful image of ugly weeds on a grave that hint at "some hideous secret," is rooted in sound psychology: untold secrets can fester. Arthur's argument, by contrast, is grounded in the historical fact that closing confessionals turned whole generations to rituals of corporate repentance and, in the case of the Puritans, to more highly crafted strategies of repentance like written spiritual autobiographies. Even sermons may encode personal contrition in exegetical and homiletical discourse, serving, perhaps, to unburden the preacher without altogether disclosing secrets the listeners might find unsettling. The relative claims of theology and psychology are held in tension throughout this story: Hawthorne appears to have found the two somewhat at odds.

Finally, it appears that public confession in Arthur's case tends to backfire. On occasion he ventures timidly to allude to his own sinfulness in the pulpit—dipping his toe in the water, as it were. Perhaps because of his tentativeness, the attempt simply reinforces his congregation's inclination to make him into the saint they want him to be:

> More than once . . . he had told his hearers that he was altogether vile, a viler companion of the vilest, the worst of sinners, an abomination, a thing of unimaginable iniquity, and that the only wonder was that they did not see his wretched body shrivelled up before their eyes by the burning wrath of the Almighty! Could there be plainer speech than this? Would not the people start up in their seats, by a simultaneous impulse, and tear him down out of the pulpit which he defiled? Not so, indeed! They heard it all, and did but reverence him the more. They little guessed

what deadly purport lurked in those self-condemning words. "The godly youth!" said they among themselves. "The saint on earth! Alas! if he discern such sinfulness in his own white soul, what horrid spectacle would he behold in thine or mine!" The minister well knew—subtle, but remorseful hypocrite that he was!—the light in which his vague confession would be viewed. He had striven to put a cheat upon himself by making the avowal of a guilty conscience, but had gained only one other sin, and a self-acknowledged shame, without the momentary relief of being self-deceived. He had spoken the very truth, and transformed it into the veriest falsehood. And yet, by the constitution of his nature, he loved the truth, and loathed the lie, as few men ever did. Therefore, above all things else, he loathed his miserable self!

This failure to achieve a full and valid confession raises the question of what it takes for a confession to be either adequate or effective. Truth telling is harder than we think, and remorse a poor substitute for authentic repentance. Creatures whose hearts are deceitful, and perhaps especially those whose intelligence and sensitivity render them capable of compounding that deceit can, it appears, hardly find their way out of the thickets of self-subversion that seem here to mire Arthur in ambivalence and self-loathing. When, at length, he and Hester meet in the forest out of sight of their ignorant neighbors, Arthur seizes the moment to confess the agony of his isolation. His outcry provides a characteristically eloquent rationale for confession as necessary to spiritual health:

> Happy are you, Hester, that wear the scarlet letter openly upon your bosom! Mine burns in secret! Thou little knowest what a relief it is, after the torment of a seven years' cheat, to look into an eye that recognises me for what I am! Had I one friend—or were it my worst enemy!—to whom, when sickened with the praises of all other men, I could daily betake myself, and be known as the vilest of all sinners, methinks my soul might keep itself alive thereby. Even thus much of truth would save me! But not, it is all falsehood—all emptiness!—all death!

What Arthur recognizes and acknowledges at this moment with whole-hearted faith is that the truth, even the awful truth, will set us free. St. Paul's promise in 1 Cor 13:12, "Then I shall know even as also I am known," speaks to the kind of longing Arthur confesses here. To be known, acknowledged, recognized, and even judged by God is fundamentally life-giving. Cut off from that connection, one begins, even in this world, to die slowly, circling a personal hell of one's own making. After Arthur's ambiguous death scene the narrator muses, "Among many morals which press upon us from the poor minister's miserable experience, we put only this into a sentence:—'Be true! Be true! Be true! Show freely to the world, if not your worst, yet some trait whereby the worst may be inferred!'"

But the worst is not, apparently, inferred, in Arthur's case. His final confession (veiled in indirect discourse) leaves his hearers even more perversely convinced of his sanctity. Having invested heavily in making him their local saint, they see in his emaciated body not the result of wracking guilt, but the effects of pious self-immolation. They hear in his self-condemnation only the scruples of an exquisitely sensitive soul who has chosen humbly to identify with the chief of sinners. In a culminating moment unforgettable for its withheld satisfaction (some would see it as our narrator's final cruel joke on readers) Arthur rips away his shirt front to expose to the horrified public gaze . . . what? We don't know. Because "it were irreverent to describe that revelation." Really. So if that's the denouement (literally) we were hoping for, we have been sorely deceived. We don't get to know.

Moreover, whatever it was (and years of teaching this scene have yielded many an entertaining speculation) still does not serve to set at rest public uncertainty about Arthur's sin. "After many days," the narrator tells us, "when time sufficed for the people to arrange their thoughts in reference to the foregoing scene, there was more than one account of what had been witnessed on the scaffold." Most apparently saw a scarlet letter suspiciously like Hester's. (Why are we not surprised?) But did that convince them of his sin? No—rather it thrust them into a frenzy of inventive explanations designed above all things to exonerate and protect the reputation of their beloved pastor. This outcome must indeed have taken much "arrangement of thought." Rationalization takes time. If the story imparts a lesson about confession, it seems to be this: public utterance depends as much upon the disposition and intentions of the listener as upon one's own (inevitably mixed) motivations. What is revealed may just remain concealed in a new guise. Our only hope, therefore (and this is not all bad news) is that we may be heard by the God who knows our hearts, because words in this fallen world are unreliable arbiters of truth.

In light of all these complications, it would appear at least plausible that Arthur chose the lesser evil when he held his peace, and even that his greatest act of heroism lay therein, rather than in his desperate final gesture. His character seems likely to have been shaped by Hawthorne's own tendency to keep his own counsel about many things; the taciturn author mystified his own townspeople who reputedly thought him very like "an angel," but who seems to have regarded himself as rather more like Arthur—or Hester.

And what of Hester's own resistance to confession? Her sin is unavoidably public in Pearl, the "living hieroglyphic, in which was revealed the secret they so darkly sought to hide." Just as public are her many acts of conciliation, if not penance: she humbles herself, wears her "badge of shame," performs works of mercy, and lives a life of outward compliance with law and custom. But she does not confess. She neither verbally acknowledges the sinfulness of her adultery, nor obeys the order to identify the father, nor bows to the authorities who deem her an unfit mother: "'God gave her into my keeping!' she insists, as we remember. 'I will not give her up!'" Confession and compliance would be for her a form of suicide.

Indeed, Hester's refusal to confide in these "worthies" directly parallels her refusal to confide in Roger, who demands only the name of her lover for his satisfaction. Though she acquiesces to Roger's demand that she keep his secret as she keeps Arthur's, hoping that in doing so she is "rescuing [Arthur] from a blacker ruin than had overwhelmed herself," she eventually repents that compliance and tells the truth to the one person to whom she believes she owes it. To the others, she becomes convinced, she does not owe disclosures they would be sure to exploit in order to reinforce their own dubious claims to authority. She considers them no more worthy of her confidence and trust than Roger is. In both cases she challenges the men's rights to her secrets, declaring a spiritual independence of worldly (male) authority. The declaration is rooted in her own understanding of the nature of divine authority and her divine right, as it were, to mother her own child despite its illegitimacy. For her, that claim trumps all others, including that of civil law.

Nor does the narrator leave much doubt as to the effects Hester's capitulation and confession might have: Roger would wreak revenge on Arthur; Hester would lose custody of her child and (we are assured) swell the ranks of witches in the forest; the town would be scandalized and public life disrupted—or, more likely, she, like Cassandra, would simply be dismissed as a liar. Little good, it appears, would come of a complete confession. And much seems finally to come of holding her peace and guarding the secrets of her troubled heart.

Even her hesitation to tell her sad story to her daughter raises the vexed question every parent faces about what children can hear and bear. There are truths, most would agree, that would do more harm than good to the very young. Yet there is a cost to concealing them, as well. Hester considers making Pearl her confidante:

> But now the idea came strongly into Hester's mind, that Pearl, with her remarkable precocity and acuteness, might already have approached the age when she could have been made a friend, and intrusted with as much of her mother's sorrows as could be imparted, without irreverence either to the parent or the child.

So Hester resists the temptation to open her heart to Pearl, even as Pearl's insistence grows more emphatic. A spiraling tension between them comes to one climax in exactly the kind of standoff many parents have come to when the chasm that separates adults from the children whose innocence they hope to protect seems unbridgeable. Driven to literal distraction by Pearl's insistent queries, "What does the scarlet letter mean?" and "Why does the minister keep his hand over his heart?" she resorts to a punishment that precisely replicates her own interior acts of repression: "Mother!—Mother!—Why does the minister keep his hand over his heart?" "Hold thy tongue, naughty child!" answered her mother, with an asperity that she had never permitted to herself before. "Do not tease me; else I shall put thee into the dark closet!" Her decision offers a parallel to Arthur's in withholding from his congregation information that, though they might seem to have some right to it, might also do them harm.

This precarious ambivalence comes to a head in chapter 13, "Another View of Hester," which, lying at the geographical center of the story, offers a view of Hester's interior life so intimate and tragic, it seems to lift a narrative veil and afford us a glimpse of the author's own spiritual struggles. "Was existence worth accepting . . . ?" she wonders. And, going further down that dark path, she ponders the merits of suicide and infanticide as exit strategies from a world that offers little hospitality or understanding and a society that seems to have foreclosed human sympathies with labels and judgment that also forefend unwelcome truths. Hester confesses to no one because there is no one able or willing to receive her confession. Her isolation "withers" her in visible ways, but frees her as well, and this, the narrator implies, is precisely the predicament of Protestant spirituality: the mind is freed, but into isolation. Institutional abuses are redressed, but the excesses of intellectualism and individualism that are its own dark side provide little healing for broken hearts. "Thus Hester Prynne, whose heart had lost its regular and healthy throb, wandered without a clue in the dark labyrinth of mind," and minds, left to themselves, can be dangerous, even death-dealing, instruments.

The empathetic note in this remarkable chapter for the pain of Hester's intellectual and spiritual isolation gives us a sense of the narrator and a "view of Hester" unlike any other. It reads as both a manifesto and a plea for another reformation that might liberate the spirit of both men and women from institutional forms that have become prisons. Those include not only the church, but systems built on scapegoating, subjugation, unjust codes of law controlled by men who protect their power, and what we would now call "socially constructed" gender roles. "As a first step," to renewal, Hester reflects, without much hope of ever seeing such a step be taken, "the whole system of society is to be torn down and built up anew." Until women are accredited, her reasoning suggests, until the language of intellect and the testimonies of feeling can find an equal hearing in the governance of communities, until we can find ways to meet human frailty and need with compassion larger than the fear that drives punitive policies, the invitation to tell the truth will ring hollow to those whose truths fail to reinforce structures of power.

But there is another, far more personal, reason Hester cannot confess —one we are told she hid even from herself, though it "struggled out of her heart, like a serpent from its hole." She harbored some hope that at the bar of final judgment, she and Arthur, her partner in sin, might "make that their marriage-altar, for a joint futurity of endless retribution."

Hawthorne's most troubled and troubling critique of the church as he knew it—that acting as arbiter of moral law, it may have missed the point. It seems in this story to serve neither Arthur nor Roger nor Hester at the level of their deepest needs, nor to have conveyed to Pearl a hospitality that might have kept her in her birthplace among her mother's people rather than condemning her to exile because they could make no place for the illegitimate.

These excommunicant keepers of secrets may be, ironically, the most faithful truth tellers in the story, willing to tell only those truths that are likely to be heard in a context of love and understood in larger than legal terms. Their predicament is not unlike that of Jesus' disciples who, most conspicuously in the Gospel of Mark, are bearers of a secret that makes them both outsiders and insiders.[1] The narrator, doubtless echoing the author in this, if we are to judge from the record of Hawthorne's own spiritual struggles, seems to suggest that it is nearly impossible in this fallen world, and especially in a religious culture of hidebound legalism, to utter a true confession or to make "confessing our sins one to another" an efficacious act of reconciliation and healing. Peter's poignant query of Jesus, "To whom else shall we go?" comes to mind here: confession is perilous, human forgiveness contingent and uncertain, motives mixed, and language contaminated with associations that render it less fit for truth telling. So if we are to "confess our sins one to another," we would do well to seek out those souls and circumstances that can tolerate the kind of truth that sets us free. They seem to be rare. We may not find them inside institutional walls. But the note of hope here is that they will be sent, and that there will eventually be, as our narrator beautifully imagines, a "light that is to reveal all secrets, and the daybreak that shall unite all who belong to one another." The call to confession, rightly seen, is a call to the kind of community that recognizes sinners as kin who belong to one another, so deeply invested in each other's welfare that nothing can separate them from the love that has called them into life and into community, and that comes from an inexhaustible source.

---

1. For a lively discussion of this point, see Juel, *Gospel of Mark*.

-6-

Into the Wilderness

*Then was Jesus led up of the Spirit into the wilderness
to be tempted of the devil.*

MATTHEW 4:1

ONE OF THE MORE dramatic moments in *The Scarlet Letter* occurs
when, having met Arthur in the seclusion of the forest after seven
years of steady renunciation, Hester undoes the clasp that holds her badge
in place, flings it aside, and, reaching up, removes the cap that confines
her hair and lets it fall about her shoulders, "dark and rich, with at once
a shadow and a light in its abundance, and imparting the charm of softness to her features." It is a transformative moment: her smile becomes
"radiant and tender," her pale cheek glows "crimson," and she appears
to retrieve "her sex, her youth, and the whole richness of her beauty."
Miraculously, or magically, or perhaps only apparently, the forest around
her is transformed as well, as if, the narrator rhapsodizes, "the gloom of
the earth and sky had been but the effluence" of Hester's and Arthur's
hearts, vanishing with their sudden release from sorrow and constraint:

> All at once, as with a sudden smile of heaven, forth burst the sunshine, pouring a very flood into the obscure forest, gladdening each green leaf, transmuting the yellow fallen ones to gold, and gleaming adown the gray trunks of the solemn trees. The objects that had made a shadow hitherto, embodied the brightness now.

Somber cleric and sober penitent are suddenly endowed with an erotic vitality that melts away the hagiographic veneer and turns this moral tale into a love story. The climactic encounter recalls a whole chivalric tradition of virtuous love rewarded, until we pause to remember that these are no chaste maiden and her knight, but unconfessed sinners sharing their illicit secret in a place outside the precincts of moral authority, where witches meet and the "Black Man" wanders with his bloody book. Nor is the forest, for all its "sympathy" the same "green world" where Shakespeare's Rosalind and Orlando learned less costly lessons about love, but a "moral wilderness," dark, changeable, and treacherous, our narrator might say, as the human heart. The moment is not one of triumph but an apotheosis of the wrenching ambiguity that brings the lovers, and us, to a place where moral categories are no longer quite so reliable, where law seems a mockery that thwarts the very virtue it purports to protect, and where smiling heaven itself seems to bless the breaking of its own revealed statutes.

Dubbed by one critic "Calvin's ironic stepchild,"[1] Hawthorne brings a theological worldview to bear on the natural world without a theologian's commitment to resolving the question of their relationship. He shares not only with near contemporaries like Emerson, Wordsworth, and Thoreau but also, in a different and more troubled way, with Jonathan Edwards, a view of "Nature," as a testing ground for human cognitive structures and moral categories and as a measure of moral goodness. This last was the most radical, since it implied a critique of the notion of civilization as progress and progress as enlightenment or increase of virtue. Certainly the implication that "Nature" offered a readable, though arcane, instructional text comparable to Scripture flew in the face of the popularized Calvinist notion of the depravity of "natural" or unredeemed humankind. Displacing that was a highly idealistic premise of original innocence and the power of introspection, reflection, and intuition to restore us to that original state. A rough equation between the good, the innocent, and the

---

1. Donohue, *Hawthorne*.

natural eventually emerged, partly through his agency, as a defining feature of American romanticism. The questions he and his cohort raised
as a legacy to generations to come emerge in high relief in *The Scarlet
Letter*: What are we to learn from the natural world? How does it speak
to us? How does God speak to us in it or through it? What is the relationship of nature to Scripture as a source of revelation? Can we derive
moral law from observing nature? Will it teach us to be good? Are we to
regard ourselves primarily as natural creatures or as creatures set apart
by a supernaturally ordained destiny and therefore fundamentally different from other sentient beings? What is "natural man"? Do our highly
codified systems of moral and civil law run with the grain of our human
nature, or against it?

With all due respect to the foundational importance of Emerson's
essays and the prophetic force of *Walden*, as well as to the significant
body of theological writing that came from that remarkable generation,
it was in fiction that Hawthorne found the medium perfectly suited to
what the Transcendentalists declared to be the task of the preachers, wise
men, and moral guides: to teach "not so much [by] moral instruction as
moral impression."[2] "What is the office of a Christian minister?" Emerson
asked in one rhetorical outburst, and then, characteristically, proceeded
to answer his own question: "'Tis his to show the beauty of the moral
laws of the Universe . . . , to see the creation with a new eye, to behold
what he thought unorganized, crystallize into form, to see the stupendous
temple uplift its awful form, towers on towers into infinite space, echoing
all with rapturous hymns."[3] The imaginative "method" had become by
1850 a standard homiletic practice; William Ware's sermons, for instance,
focused heavily on imaginative interpolation of emotional content into
biblical stories, designed to induce empathetic understanding that would
lead to theological reflection.[4] On the other hand, fiction had a bad name
among even these liberal neo-Calvinists. Fiction, for this rather earnest
lot, had to be didactic to justify its place on the shelves with weightier
tomes. Even "religious" novels were suspect. This prejudice resulted in
an intellectual dilemma that drove wordsmiths to seek highly original
modes of discourse that might offer a way to tell truth appropriately

2. Ralph Waldo Emerson, a sermon preached in Brooklyn, Connecticut, at the instal-
lation of the Rev. Samuel Joseph May, quoted in Buell, *Literary Transcendentalism*, 107.

3. Buell, ibid., 106.

4. Ibid., 109.

"slant." Certainly Hawthorne's "romances" with their cryptic "hieroglyph-ics" were a consummate achievement of this kind. Their strong appeal to imagination and "fancy" is equaled by an equally complex appeal to moral sensibilities. What Ellery Channing said about Thoreau might eas-ily have been said about Hawthorne—that "His temperament is so moral, his least observation will breed a sermon."[5]

Because he described himself as merely a writer of "romances," and therefore less bound than some of his seminary-trained contemporaries to the terms of either theological or philosophical debate, Hawthorne made very free not only with the terms and concepts of those debates, but also with his attitude toward the whole enterprise of truth-seeking. His focus upon place is key to his insistent relativization of moral rea-soning about human experience. Our apprehension of truth, he insists, is never context-free. We may finally be unable to distinguish the inner from the outer landscape, so enmeshed are we in the web of conscience and consciousness.

The "where" in this story, therefore, is crucial to its meaning. To set a scene was to frame a particular set of questions that derived their shape and meaning from that frame, since all questions arise only in a theater of action. Not only is behavior bound by context, Hawthorne suggests, but moral reasoning itself arises out of a context of encounter with God, others, self, or the natural world. The three settings that figure in the story—town, seashore, and forest—are so fraught with symbolic signifi-cance that the question "where" assumes the same importance as "why" in fathoming characters' motives and actions.

To be in the town, especially for Hester and Arthur, was to be in the presence and under the often judgmental surveillance of other inhabit-ants. In numerous scenes the town is depicted as a crowded place; people gather to see Hester walk to the scaffold, to applaud the young minister as he processes toward the pulpit for his election day sermon, to taunt moth-er and child as they pass through, to witness the minister's final hour. The town is essentially a theater, and the populace a "chorus" like those in ancient Greek tragedy. In the town law and custom regulate action, and the "secrets of the heart," which the narrator clearly regards as the more significant dimension of human stories, remain hidden because there is no safe or acceptable way to express them. Christian civilization, as it is

5. Ibid., 111.

represented here, seems to have produced a deep division between public and private self—a division whose consequences are often chronic guilt or ingrained hypocrisy. A question that arises in the context of town life, therefore, is whether honesty is possible among people so constrained by doctrine and dogma taught without direct reference to experience and punitively enforced.

Hester's field of action is largely the town, but the story takes us to two other places where her portrait is more intimately drawn: the seashore and the forest. Her cottage at the seashore occupies liminal space, neither wholly in nor out of the town's precincts and the range of public gaze. Her place is marginal in every sense, and her physical situation works as an "emblem" of her metaphysical condition. She is neither wholly under the governance of church and state nor wholly free of them. She submits by her own volition to their orders, leaving her cottage daily to travel among the townsfolk and serve them in a way reminiscent of Jesus' ministry among the crowds between his periods of retreat to the wilderness and solitude. But it is at the seashore that she works out her own salvation, constructing the terms of her own isolated existence. There she considers the compromises necessary to raising a child, whose days are spent largely at play in the mute but endlessly suggestive natural world.

For the first two-thirds of the book the forest remains as a rather ominous backdrop to the action. Roger emerges from it in the company of a "red man"—an association that lends him a certain authority and fascination but also makes him an object of suspicion. Mistress Hibbens invites Hester to a gathering, presumably of witches, in the forest. Stories of the forest as the realm of the "Black Man," though Hawthorne, surrounded by abolitionists, can't have overlooked the edgy irony of that common way of referring to the devil, identify it as a demonically inhabited place of evil, to be entered with trepidation and only on compelling errands. The forest is associated with darkness, hiddenness, labyrinthine, winding paths, the presumably lawless and violent life of "savages," lush and erotic "luxuriance," and depths in which one might easily lose one's way, never to return. This all remains a secondary frame to the action until, seven years into Hester's life of penitence and sixteen chapters into the narrative, the story shifts to forest scenes in which the issues represented in the individual tales of each of the four main characters are most sharply defined and complicated.

Hester has by this point made her accommodations to the community, but continues to feel responsible for Dimmesdale. She seeks a time and place to warn him about Chillingworth's vengeful intentions, and chooses the forest as safest from others' scrutiny. Dimmesdale had gone to "visit the apostle Eliot, among his Indian converts." The historical John Eliot was the first to preach to the native peoples in their own dialects and became known as "Apostle to the Indians." This journey of Dimmesdale's takes him outside the fold of his own flock, into a precarious and alien world. The road both he and Hester take into the "primeval forest" was "no other than a footpath," and the forest is so black and dense, we are told (lest we miss the analogy), that "it imaged not amiss the moral wilderness in which [Hester] had so long been wandering." The somber weather deepens the natural darkness and seems, along with other meteorological effects, to impart meaning to the events that play out among the trees. Both sunlight and gloom are allegorized as emblems of the dark and light spirits of Hester and her child, but are also personified in such a way as to suggest that every element of nature is not only a sentient but an intelligent presence, capable of intention and responsive to human action and even veiled motive. Thus the "sportive" sunlight "withdrew itself as they came nigh," willfully, it seems, abandoning them to the darkness that so befits and mirrors Hester's inner turmoil. Pearl seems to draw sunlight to her as Hester drives it away. She seems to Hester actually to "catch the sunshine": "The light lingered about the lonely child, as if glad of such a playmate, until her mother had drawn almost nigh enough to step into the magic circle too."

Fascinated with contemporary theories of attraction and emanation, animal magnetism and animism, Hawthorne raises in passages like these questions about what we might call the economy of energy shared by humans and other natural creatures. Pearl's character, as yet largely unformed by human influence, and strangely resistant even to her mother's, seems completely in harmony with the natural world. Throughout the book she is associated with birds, flowers, water, and dancing light. Recalling Emerson's often-quoted observation that "beauty is its own excuse for being," Pearl, too, seems her own excuse for being—self-contained, *sui generis*. She seems to contain some independent growth principle that makes a mockery of her elders' efforts to "train her up in the way she should go." This highly Romantic notion of childhood, a condition of primordial innocence lost in the process of acculturation, lends itself nicely to a more comprehensive theory of human nature that runs quite at odds with Calvinist doctrine, suggesting namely that untaught and unredeemed nature is not depraved, but "natural," and as such, amoral. Pearl is never an "angelic" child, but an elf-child, an imp child, a fairy child, a sprite—all creatures that represent a pagan and essentially amoral world. To read these images didactically, as the tale begs to be read, is to recognize in Pearl's character a flagrant critique of conventional moral training which denatures us or, in orienting us toward a God outside nature, literally disorients us to the natural world, and makes us unfit and uncomfortable to dwell in it. What if to be natural were to be neither good nor evil? In Pearl we see a portrait of innocence ingenious in its logic: the innocence lost when we enter and submit to the world of moral consciousness is not a state of angelic goodness, but a state of wildness, freedom, accord between self and nature, and spontaneity. It is precisely Pearl's unclassifiability in moral terms that makes her such a threat to both her parents and to the whole hierarchy of townspeople, from the governor and chief clerics to the Puritan children who propose to fling mud at her when she walks by.

One manifestation of this innocence is Pearl's open curiosity about what she senses to be hidden, secret, or taboo. Cryptic herself, she nevertheless speaks a language more honest than those around her, and persistently tries to rip open the veil of pretense in their words. Thus she undermines the questions of the catechism by a deft refusal to understand or accept the terms of the questions and by the symbolic precision in her pregnant answers. Thus, too, she badgers Hester to tell her more about the "Black Man":

> How he haunts this forest, and carries a book with him a big, heavy book, with iron clasps; and how this ugly Black Man offers his book and an iron pen to everybody that meets him here among the trees; and they are to write their names with their own blood and then he sets his mark on their bosoms.

Pearl has the story from "the old dame in the chimney-corner" in a house where Hester kept watch. It is lore passed in secret, and even, it is suggested, through devious means, since Pearl reports, the old woman "fancied me asleep while she was talking of it," implying, we infer, that some information needs to be, or may only be, transmitted via the unconscious. Innocently, and relentlessly, she continues her pursuit of the painful subject:

> She said that a thousand and a thousand people had met him here,
> and had written in his book, and have his mark on them. And that
> ugly tempered lady, old Mistress Hibbens, was one. And, mother,
> the old dame said that this scarlet letter was the Black Man's mark
> on thee, and that it glows like a red flame when thou meetest him
> at midnight, here in the dark wood.

Pearl's absence of fear adds to her innocence a sense of her invulnerability to evil simply because it does not exist for her as a category, and strangely recalls Paul's admonition to scrupulous Christians, "To the pure all things are pure" (Titus 1:15), purity here represented as being untainted by the guilt, denial, and hypocrisy that are products of an overwrought conscience denatured by legalism. The "Black Man," of course, converges ironically with the figure of Arthur, clad in clerical garb, as he appears just in time to interrupt her little colloquy. It is hard not to smile at Hester's emphatic correction as the clergyman comes into view: "It is no Black Man! . . . It is the minister."

Said minister arrives to find them seated "on a luxuriant heap of moss; which, at some epoch of the preceding century, had been a gigantic pine, with its roots and trunk in the darksome shade, and its head aloft in the atmosphere." Sentences like this one, which abound, are emphatic reminders that nothing in the natural world is simply what it is at the moment we happen to look upon it, but one manifestation of an ongoing process of change—life, decay, rebirth. Every tree Hester touches is a record and a vestige, and the very soil under her feet a silent and cryptic text in which is embedded a past that is larger than human history. Human history, indeed, pales into insignificance beside the great natural cycles that belie its myths of progress. Like the trees, foliage, and compost, the brook that flows at Hester's feet is also a manifestation of change, not of metamorphic cycles, but of the work of accident and adaptation:

> A brook [flowed] through the midst, over a bed of fallen and
> drowned leaves. The trees impending over it had flung down
> great branches, from time to time, which choked up the current,
> and compelled it to form eddies and black depths at some points;
> while, in its swifter and livelier passages, there appeared a channel-
> way of pebbles, and brown, sparkling sand. . . . All these giant
> trees and boulders of granite seemed intent on making a mystery
> of the course of this small brook; fearing, perhaps, that with its
> never-ceasing loquacity, it should whisper tales out of the heart
> of the old forest whence it flowed, or mirror its revelations on the

smooth surface of a pool. Continually, indeed, as it stole onward, the streamlet kept up a babble, kind, quiet, soothing, but melancholy, like the voice of a young child that was spending its infancy without playfulness, and knew not how to be merry among sad acquaintance and events of somber hue.

Lest we miss the allegorical possibilities, our kind narrator spells them out for us. Not only may the brook symbolize the flow of time and change, the course of story and history, but also it reflects, like the sunlight, the character of Pearl, for whom every natural feature she looks upon becomes a mirror and a measure:

Pearl resembled the brook, inasmuch as the current of her life gushed from a well-spring as mysterious, and had flowed through scenes shadowed as heavily with gloom. But, unlike the little stream, she danced and sparkled, and prattled airily along her course.

Given what we have seen about Pearl's almost mystical communion with nature, the question she puts to her mother seems to demand to be taken as more than a childish tendency to personification: "What does this sad little brook say, mother?" and her mother takes it thus seriously: "'If thou hadst a sorrow of thine own, the brook might tell thee of it,' answered her mother, 'even as it is telling me of mine!'" Hester's outcast state and relative freedom from the social and mental constraints that bound her to a civilized worldview have given her some play of mind that allows her to enter into Pearl's mode of understanding in this way, and at least to humor her whimsical assignment of subjectivity and significance to the creatures around her with an equally imaginative response.

The pathetic fallacy dominates long ensuing descriptions of the forest, lending animation to every stirring leaf and passing breeze, intention to every visual pattern, and meaning to every sound. The natural environment becomes supercharged with Presence that gives it "charm" in a very literal sense, and the creatures of the forest seem in subtle communion with each other, just beyond the reach of the humans' understanding: "one solemn old tree groaned dolefully to another, as if telling the sad story of the pair that sat beneath, or constrained to forbode evil to come." The implied fancy that the trees' discourse is about their own story is a touching, even amusing, allusion to our very human tendency to project our own concerns outward, thus preventing our receiving, and learning from, the otherness of the creatures around us. Hawthorne's skepticism about the extreme immanentism of the Transcendentalists comes through clearly in passages like this one, where self-preoccupation, not to say a certain mild paranoia, dominates perception.

Conveniently, Pearl wanders away from her mother upon Arthur's appearance, leaving the narrator free to conjure the scene as a meeting of "our first parents" in the garden. The equation of forest with garden is a curious but common one among colonial American writers, ideally suited to Hawthorne's purposes. Here the Adam and Eve story may be retold and recast, about a man and a woman once again hidden among the leaves, fearfully speculating about the consequences of their lost innocence. Overlaid on the primordial tale is a vision of the future adumbrated in this meeting of guilt-laden souls:

> So strangely did they meet, in the dim wood, that it was like the first encounter, in the world beyond the grave, of two spirits who had been intimately connected in their former life, but now stood coldly shuddering, in mutual dread, as not yet familiar with their state, nor wonted to the companionship of disembodied beings. Each a ghost, and awe-stricken at the other ghost!

In both cases the element of apprehensive, if not horrified, mutual recognition and shared guilt is the same. In both cases the characters inhabit a world apart, their drama having little to do with the worldly realm to which they do not yet—or do not any longer—belong.

As Hester and Arthur walk deeper into the forest, their conversation takes them likewise "step by step, into the themes that were brooding deepest in their hearts." A descent into the depths, of course, in any literary context, has enormous symbolic valence. Depth is a metaphor that has to do with a particular kind of vulnerability—to being overwhelmed, immersed, drowned, even dissolved. In depth psychology the word has to do with penetrating the layers of the psyche from outer world-consciousness to the innermost regions of self-knowing into the very heart of the mystery of selfhood where, as some of Hawthorne's Transcendentalist contemporaries believed, Self dwells with God. Yeats refers to the "deep heart's core" as the receptor of knowledge beyond rational grasp, a place of awareness so subtle that to enter it is to leave the world of ordinary reference and embark on a private and perilous journey. Here the forest path is the winding way of that journey inward. Hester and Arthur know the forest; even so they are unsettled, aware of not "belonging" there— certainly not in the sanguine and serene way that Pearl belongs. They are set apart from nature by their consciousness of themselves as sinful creatures, sin being in their world the defining act that sets humans apart from the rest of creation, and in relation to a redeeming God. But it is also their sinfulness that leads them back into the forest to seek its shelter, as if it is the civilized world and not the "wilds" from which they need protection. As, indeed, it is. It is the law that condemns them, and nature, our theologically subversive narrator suggests, might heal them, nature being beyond the laws of man. Here they might, in a sense, be "born again," redeemed by a return to a state of natural innocence. A gospel without Christ, to be sure, and therefore a hope blasphemous in its presumption, but a suggestion that surely sharpens the question of the role of nature in bringing us "back" to ourselves, "back" from the waywardness of our own misplaced fantasies of dominion over the earth, "back" to a world we did not make, as creatures, not conquerors or controllers.

Hester and Arthur try, by fiat, to proclaim themselves free of human law and release themselves into a state of consciousness in which humans are governed only by the laws of nature and "the heart," the latter being a conveniently ambiguous term for the leadings of what might variously be the Holy Spirit, love, animal attraction, or lust. Reframed under the rubric of those laws, their love assumes a luminous and unique character of wholeness and honesty that cannot be recognized when it is regarded as sin. Momentarily Arthur has an epiphany that releases him from the bondage of his usual forms of judgment: "Here, seen only by her eyes, Arthur Dimmesdale, false to God and man, might be, for one moment, true!" And Hester insists, "What we did had a consecration of its own," but even in her insistence seems to protest too much. Ultimately they take the "dreary" forest path that leads "backwards to the settlement," but only after Hester points out that it "leads onwards, too!" The lovers' inability finally to throw off the shackles of moral and ecclesiastical legalism and reenter a state of nature recalls the disbelief of Nicodemus' incredulous question about innocence regained: "But how shall I be born again? Shall a man enter a second time into his mother's womb . . . ?" (John 3:4). It recalls, too, the very real presence of peoples of the forest who to the colonists represented that benighted but somehow enviable state, and the combined attraction and fear many felt for a life that some, at least, suspected was not wholly unenlightened, despite ignorance of the gospel. To "go native," a term many European explorers used to describe the gradual loss of their own cultural frames of reference and adaptation to native cultures, was a prospect that held both fascination and fear for many settlers. Once the possibility was allowed that the "savages" might in fact be privy to their own forms of enlightenment a frightening relativizing of what had been held to be absolute had almost inevitably to take place. At this point in the story, Hester's values have already been thus relativized. She dwells in paradox, clinging for a variety of reasons, primarily her concern for raising Pearl, to the structures of Christian faith and theocratic social order while at the same time entertaining unabashedly her own attraction to both witchcraft and native life—in other words, to the possibility of joining the "other sheep" outside the fold. The biblical image of domesticated sheep in a fold is useful to recall in this context as a way the Christian colonists were accustomed to thinking of themselves and their position in the world: chosen, protected, dependent, to be sure, but privileged in their dependency. To leave the fold was to be devoured by wolves. So domesticity and wildness became analogues for salutary obedience to divine ordinance, and dangerous, willful ignorance of the way of grace. But Hester (or, more to the point, our narrator) confuses this neat dichotomy by valorizing the way of the wild as the way of nature, and so in keeping with the order of creation. In her effort to persuade Arthur to escape with her she cleverly reminds him that the forms of life as they know them are only a thin veneer on the face of nature, come from it, and, she might conclude, will as surely be outlived by it: "Doth the universe lie within the compass of yonder town, which only a little time ago was but a leaf-strewn desert, as lonely as this around us?" she asks, at one stroke belittling to insignificance what to him is an utterly crucial distinction between the civilized and the natural world.

Hester's second line of appeal essentially reverses the logic of her first. She invokes Arthur's missionary spirit, suggesting that if he cannot choose to leave the fold for reason of his own happiness, he might yet find a way to do so that could be brought under the rubric of God's will: "There is good to be done! Exchange this false life of thine for a true one. Be, if thy spirit summon thee to such a mission, the teacher and apostle of the red men." For a few illuminating moments Arthur opens his ear to her and hears. He opens the floodgates of emotion and imagination and enters an altered state so powerful that (we are given to believe) the forest itself is transformed. The surrounding gloom vanishes "as if [it] had been but the effluence of these two mortal hearts" and sunshine pours into the forest "as with a sudden smile of heaven, . . . gladdening each green leaf, transmuting the yellow fallen ones to gold, and gleaming adown the gray trunks of the solemn trees." Of course the characteristic "as if" clauses liberally strewn through this rhapsody throw into question the very claim made in the ensuing paragraph that "such was the sympathy of Nature—that wild, heathen Nature of the forest, never subjugated by human law, nor illumined by higher truth—with the bliss of those two spirits!" "Love," the narrator continues, "must always create a sunshine, filling the heart so full of radiance, that it overflows upon the outward world." This would seem a serious testimony to the actual transforming power of human love as a natural force of equal reality to that force "that through the green fuse drives the flower" but for the mitigating logic of the next sentence: "Had the forest still kept its gloom, it would have been bright in Hester's eyes, and bright in Arthur Dimmesdale's!" The reader is left to wonder, did the forest keep its gloom, or not? How literally are we to read this tale of transformation? What is the relationship posited here between the physical and the spiritual worlds? Does nature participate in the movements of the spirit or vice versa? Are we absorbent or radiant beings —and if both, how are we to know ourselves except as Aeolean harps? Hawthorne reverts to these questions as matters of endless speculation, and not frivolous, since the questions themselves provide some check on both anthropomorphic inflation and the self-obliterating extremes of predestinarian logic. In this scene, in any case, the transformation does not last. Here again some allusion may be inferred to the biblical scene of Jesus' transfiguration—a momentary lifting of the veil to reveal what cannot be lastingly experienced on this earth—an intersection of natural and supernatural being defying the ordering categories of human experience as we know it and must live it out. So here, what is envisioned cannot, finally, be acted on within the parameters of the logic of these characters and the fates they have been cast.

Arthur cannot finally rise to Hester's challenge. His "nature" has so given way to "culture" that he is no longer capable of entertaining for more than a fleeting moment the thought of living outside the structures that so bind and define him. His excitement in that one moment has something superficial and precarious in it, almost like a hyperventilation of the spirit: "a glow of strange enjoyment threw its flickering brightness over the trouble of his breast. It was the exhilarating effect—upon a prisoner just escaped from the dungeon of his own heart—of breathing the wild, free atmosphere of an unredeemed, unchristianized, lawless region." It is too strong a tonic for him in his overrefined and therefore weakened state.

Arthur's development over seven years has taken him further into the refinements of scrupulosity, mental isolation, theological ratiocination. He has become etherealized, in touch with the world around him almost exclusively by means of the spoken and written word, and except for the painful secret he carries in his heart, barely in touch with his own pale body. Hester, on the other hand, has increasingly habituated herself to the "lawlessness" of the natural world, and to her state of excommunication. The latter seems in fact to have opened the way to a deeper communion with nature; the very terms in which her spiritual life is described attribute high significance to her "naturalization" in the wild, unchristianized world:

> She had wandered, without rule or guidance, in a moral wilderness; as vast, as intricate and shadowy, as the untamed forest, amid the gloom of which they were now holding a colloquy that was to decide their fate. Her intellect and heart had their home, as it were, in desert places, where she roamed as freely as the wild Indian in his woods. For years past she had looked from this estranged point of view at human institutions, and whatever priests or legislators had established; criticizing all with hardly more reverence than the Indian would feel for the clerical band, the judicial robe, the pillory, the gallows, the fireside, or the church. The tendency of her fate and fortunes had been to set her free. The scarlet letter was her passport into regions where other women dared not tread.

The resemblances between Hester's story and that of Jesus emerge here with particular clarity. She is "despised and rejected"; she walks the crowded ways of the village healing and, ultimately, teaching, but retreats to the wilderness for her own spiritual nourishment; she obeys men's laws with complete submission so long as doing so serves her complex purposes, but recognizes and here appeals to a higher law "written on men's hearts" and confirmed in the world of nature; she is capable of fine moral reasoning, and able to use it to confuse this custodian of moral law; she is free with a freedom that expresses itself in a paradoxical coexistence with a life of service and submission. She is not, essentially, a rebel, but a woman set apart first by her sin, and finally by her capacity to receive and live in a state of redemption that has come to her by the very agency of her punishment: banishment to the margins of society and branding with a label that finally loses its original meaning and, like language itself, fails before the natural forces of love and life that will bear no simple categorization. Living in the wilderness, she has become "wild," and, like the prophet who lived on locusts and wild honey, a prophet and reminder of what has been forgotten by most of those among whom she lives as an outsider. The forgotten thing is the essential thing: that we belong to nature, and as natural creatures, made in the image of God, we are good as nature is good; that all of nature speaks of forgiveness and rebirth as surely as it does of darkness, death, and desolation. Like numerous colonists in history, she looked at the "red man" and found the very image of the forgotten self, and in that recognition opened herself to a more inclusive vision of her own humanness.

The image of the Indian in colonial narratives, in post-revolutionary essays and political writings, in Cooper and Thoreau, and again in Hawthorne, remains consistently, provocatively ambiguous. Fraught both with actual mystery and symbolic possibility, the Indian, so called, has represented in Anglo-American writing the white man's shadow, in the Jungian sense—the embodiment of unfulfilled or unactualized desire or potential, the aspect of the self that is suppressed, hidden, denied, and so must be projected in order to be seen. Indians, like African Americans, have been signs and symbols of colonial guilt at being the oppressors, the enslavers, the expropriators. The rhetoric of colonialism leaves very little room to deal with that particular variety of guilt, so overdetermined is it by the ideology of divine mission, or, as it later became, manifest destiny.

The Indian as inhabitant of the forest, then, is doubly significant. He is a creature "acquainted with the night," whose knowledge is neither of "this world," meaning civilization, nor of the next, but of some extraneous and indeterminate realm akin, perhaps, to the liminal spheres of paganism, sorcery, or witchcraft. In Roger the two converge, his adaptation to native ways manifesting in his healing arts and deep familiarity with the powers of nature as well as in a mysterious manner and distance from the proprieties of society in favor of his own obsessive pursuits that make him that extreme opposite of the "primitive" or natural man—a Faust. It is to escape Roger's gaze, primarily, that the lovers meet in the forest, yet any moment one expects him to appear, so prone is he to inhabit wild regions. Hester asks Arthur, reaching a point of passionate impatience with his hesitations, "Is there not shade enough in all this gloomy forest to shield thee from the gaze of Roger Chillingworth?" Implied in this rhetorical outburst is not only an indictment of Arthur's timidity, but also an oblique testimony to Chillingworth's power to penetrate what is hidden, to see in the darkness of both the forest and, as we have seen prior to this, the heart. Here, as in other places, he is spoken of as having, if not supernatural powers, then at least extraordinarily acute natural ones, and one is left pondering what difference there may be between the two.

The question is the same one Pearl so often serves to raise, and it is Pearl who brings the transforming encounter in the forest to its disappointing end. "Airy sprite" that she is, she is also the force that grounds them in social reality and necessity. When Hester and Arthur finally think to look for her, they see her at a distance as a "bright-appareled vision, in a sunbeam" which "quivered to and fro, making her figure dim or distinct,—now like a real child, now like a child's spirit,—as the splendor went and came again." Later, when she throws a tantrum in response to the bewildering change in her mother's appearance without the ubiquitous letter and cap, the trees and winds "seem to lend her their sympathetic encouragement." In her parents' world but not of it, this child challenges all norms and social categories and here even the basic categories that confirm humanness. The sympathies of nature that expressed themselves so fleetingly to Arthur and Hester seem more credible in relation to her way of being, though the narrator, who always gives with one hand and takes with the other, ultimately undermines his own flight of fancy about how all the forest creatures surround and support her in recognition of a fellow creature:

> The small denizens of the wilderness hardly took pains to move out of her path . . . A wolf, it is said,—but here the tale has surely lapsed into the improbable,—came up, and smelt of Pearl's robe, and offered his savage head to be patted by her hand. The truth seems to be, however, that the mother-forest, and these wild things which it nourished, all recognized a kindred wildness in the human child.

However literal we choose to be about the representation of her relationship with the natural world, Pearl seems not unlike the feral child who in becoming wild actually becomes naturalized in a way easily confused with supernatural. Thus she has and maintains a special connection to the creatures of the forest. Arthur himself, sober cleric and judge, hardly an exemplar of fanciful imagination, muses as he watches her, "I have a strange fancy . . . that this brook is the boundary between two worlds, and that thou canst never meet thy Pearl again. Or is she an elfish spirit, who, as the legends of our childhood taught us, is forbidden to cross a running stream?" This fancy is the beginning of Arthur's retreat from epiphany. He is no longer coming to terms with the challenge this mother and child present to his capacity for actual change, but relegating them to the realm of story and dream. And indeed, as he makes his way back to the town half-crazed by the cognitive dissonance this experience has engendered, he looks back to see Hester almost as a ghost, standing by a tree, hardly visible any more. He is left, as in fairy tales, with one gift: he is able now to see more clearly into the darkness of human hearts, and walks among his townspeople acutely and miserably aware of their sins, though whether this awareness is prophecy or projection is left again to speculation.

The forest scene closes after the three have left their trysting place to return to the ambiguities of the world of men. The final word is left for the forest itself. What has transpired there has been recorded; nature is not left untouched by human intrusion, human energies, human stories, but receives the human imprint to be decoded "ages and ages hence" by other wanderers who hear the call of the wild:

> And now this fateful interview had come to a close. The dell was to be left a solitude among its dark, old trees, which, with their multitudinous tongues, would whisper long of what had passed there, and no mortal be the wiser. And the melancholy brook would add this other tale to the mystery with which its little heart was already overburdened, and whereof it still kept up a murmuring babble, with not a whit more cheerfulness of tone than for ages heretofore.

We are left wondering, which seems, in Hawthorne's psychology, where we must always be left, perplexed and awestruck before mysteries that invite exploration but defy resolution. Our relationship to nature is one of those. That it is reciprocal seems eminently clear. That there are powers, forces, and energies at work among all the creatures of the natural world our narrator does not question, and asks us to accept. That we may recognize these by nonrational means, by opening our hearts, by foregoing our need for explanation in favor of a deeper kind of experience that addresses heart rather than mind seems to be the admonition of this "sermon." And there are other messages, urgent despite their ambiguity: that the journey into the wilderness is both precarious and necessary for the development of true moral vision. That intuition must counterbalance reason if truth is to be known. That the natural world provides a challenge and corrective to the distortions and perversions we wreak upon ourselves by presuming too much upon the power we have been given to "take dominion over the earth."

-7-

Those Not Against Us

For he that is not against us is for us.

LUKE 9:50

THE FIRST CHAPTER OF Hawthorne's "tale of human frailty and sorrow" begins at a site of punishment—a prison—identified by our historian-narrator as one of the earliest and most necessary structures in any new colony, "whatever Utopia of human virtue and happiness they might originally project." Crime and punishment, that resigned philosopher implies, are inevitable wherever there is "civilization." The second chapter opens at that same site from the perspective of the expectant crowd awaiting the appearance of a prisoner. The narrator assumes one of his multiple roles, this time as uninformed outsider, and speculates about what the crowd might be anticipating:

> It might be that an Antinomian, a Quaker, or other heterodox religionist, was to be scourged out of the town, or an idle or vagrant Indian, whom the white man's firewater had made riotous about the streets, was to be driven with stripes into the shadow of the forest. It might be, too, that a witch, like old Mistress Hibbins, the bitter-tempered widow of the magistrate, was to die upon the gallows.

This telling inventory of possible malefactors succinctly delineates the pale outside of which dissenters, native peoples, and suspicious women had cause to fear for their lives. The reach and extremity of Puritan punishment, as this acerbic historian portrays it, is both fearsome and unjust. The injustice of their exclusion and punishment comes clear in the brief clauses that describe the criminals. It was, after all, "the white man's firewater" that was likely responsible for the Indians' idleness, vagrancy, or riotous behavior. And if Mistress Hibbens is a "bitter-tempered widow," one is at least led to wonder what might have so embittered her, and whether marriage to a "magistrate" might have provided some cause. Likewise, we don't have far to look in the historical record for the theological and ecclesial excesses that drove the "heterodox" into their varieties of dissent. That the narrator presumes to canonize one of those dissenters in this same chapter as the "sainted Anne Hutchinson" gives us a broad hint as to his sympathies.

Those sympathies fuel the irony that laces the narrator's many observations about Puritan law and practices. He invites us, often in subtle asides, but sometimes, as in the remarkably intimate portrait of Hester's plight in chapter 13, to consider all these outsiders in terms of mitigating circumstances, the injustice of the judgments against them, and their clear claim to inclusion in a theology that rests on Jesus' admonition to the disciples to leave those outside his fellowship alone, for "he that is not against us is for us" (Luke 9:50). This inclusive word is complicated by the other side of the paradox in the more often quoted "He that is not with me is against me" (Matt 12:30). Each provides a corrective to particular excesses. In the case of Puritan and subsequent American theologies and politics of exclusion, Hawthorne's shift of emphasis constitutes its own vigorous brand of dissent.

The heroes of heterodoxy—Anne Hutchinson, Roger Williams, John Woolman, and many others persecuted in the colonies for their alternative readings of Scripture—are held up for our consideration as victims of systematic oppression rather than as threats to civilized Christian community. So are the Indians who, even in 1850, lived in close proximity to white communities and troubled the consciences of their more thoughtful members. And even the "witches"—women who lived alone, claimed separate spheres of influence, advanced feminist causes, and challenged male hegemony—might be recognized as victims of such oppression. Readers from the dominant culture are thus compelled to take stock of their own participation in systemic injustices. Christian readers, in particular, are invited to reconsider the more exclusionary readings of the Gospel as well as the damage inflicted by the "church militant" on outsiders of every stripe. To the extent that vestiges of theocracy lingered then—and now—Hawthorne's oblique appeal has urgent political implications.

Like his neighbor, Thoreau, Hawthorne was concerned and curious about the Indians. In the quasi-autobiographical "Custom House" section of *The Scarlet Letter*, he specifically recalls "talking with Thoreau about pine-trees and Indian relics" and his own pleasure at finding Indian arrowheads "in a field near the Old Manse," and elsewhere indicates both an awareness and a sympathetic interest in the folk who seem to have appeared regularly and frequently on the periphery of New England towns. In "The Custom House," upon his discovery of the scarlet letter in an old trunk, he considers, "among other hypotheses, whether the letter might not have been one of those decorations which the white men used to contrive in order to take the eyes of Indians," calling attention to the devices and ploys settlers employed to exploit peoples they presumed to be childlike and gullible. Like many other thoughtful Americans who had witnessed Andrew Jackson's genocidal "removal" of whole native populations from their lands, he carried a burden of "white guilt" especially evident in *The House of the Seven Gables* where the theft of Indian land turns out to be a key to mysterious psycho-spiritual forces at work in the Pynchon family. In many of his stories Indians appear at the edges of the action, not as threats, but as disturbing reminders of what seemed an oxymoron to the Puritan settlers: non-Christian civilization.

The spirit that informed Benjamin Franklin's landmark essay, "Remarks Concerning the Savages of North America" seems to have provided a legacy Hawthorne could draw upon directly:

> Savages we call them, because their manners differ from ours, which we think the perfection of civility; they think the same of theirs.
>
> Perhaps, if we could examine the manners of different nations with Impartiality, we should find no People so rude, as to be without any Rules of Politeness; nor any so polite, as not to have some remains of Rudeness.
>
> The Indian Men, when young, are Hunters and Warriors; when old, Counselors; for all their Government is by Counsel, or Advice, of the sages; there is no Force, there are no Prisons, no Officers to compel Obedience, or inflict punishment. Hence they generally study Oratory; the best speaker having the most Influence.

The Indian Women till the Ground, dress the Food, nurse and bring up the Children, and preserve and hand down to posterity the Memory of Public Transactions. These Employments of Men and Women are accounted natural and honorable. Having few Artificial Wants, they have abundance of Leisure for Improvement by Conversation. Our laborious manner of Life, compared with theirs, they esteem slavish and base; and the Learning, on which we value ourselves, they regard as frivolous and useless.[1]

Representing Indian culture in terms of wise governance, fair distribution of labor, and mutual consideration, Franklin challenged deeply held prejudices that not only legitimated slaughter but protected white Europeans' sense of entitlement to the lands and resources they summarily stole. To acknowledge the equality, legitimacy, and in some respects, superiority of Indian cultures was to weaken the mandate, as many colonists understood it, to "take dominion" of American land, "improve" it, and make it a "city on a hill." Their mandate depended directly on selective readings of scriptural wilderness stories as type and analogue of their own historical situation, and upon consistently viewing the Indians as enemies. Late in the chronicle of Hester's transformation, as she becomes not only acceptable, but sanctified by her years of solitary and penitential service, local lore reports "that an Indian had drawn his arrow against the badge, and that the missile struck it, and fell harmless to the ground." Recasting her as a target of native hostilities realigns her with the community that define themselves in terms of that enmity.

Even by 1850, Hawthorne's invitation to reread Scripture in a more inclusive, open-ended way, veiled as it was behind the trappings of fiction, posed something of a political threat. The "captivity narratives" of colonists who were kidnapped and held hostage by tribal peoples in the course of local warfare often revealed remarkable complexity and even ambivalence in their representation of those they had taken to be merely "savages." Defections and intermarriage were not altogether uncommon. As they became conventionalized, one of the purposes of captivity narratives (not unlike war narratives) was to relegitimate the agenda of the white settlers. But many who reported close encounters with native peoples could not return comfortably to the simplistic notions of savages that kept these "alien" peoples safely at bay in a theological outback.

---

1. Franklin, *Autobiography and Other Writings*, 311.

Clearly, Roger Chillingworth was one of these "defectors." Though he introduces himself as having been "held in bonds among the heathen-folk" and brought to town to "be redeemed out of my captivity" by magistrates who are conferring "with the Indian sagamores respecting his ransom," his attire—a "strange disarray of civilized and savage costume"—and evident "companionship" and whispered colloquy with the Indian by his side suggest a degree of acculturation that belies the notion that he was simply held against his will. As we subsequently learn, he stayed with his captors long enough to gain

> much knowledge of the properties of native herbs and roots; nor did he conceal from his patients that these simple medicines, Nature's boon to the untutored savage, had quite as large a share of his own confidence as the European Pharmacopoeia, which so many learned doctors had spent centuries in elaborating.

As he prepares a tranquilizing potion for Hester after her ordeal on the scaffold, he reassures her confidently of the safety and potency of his medicine, a gift from tribal practitioners who were willing both to share their secrets and to learn the white man's science: "I have learned many new secrets in the wilderness," he tells her, pouring a drink for her from a flask, "and here is one of them—a recipe that an Indian taught me, in requital of some lessons of my own, that were as old as Paracelsus." Interestingly, Hawthorne's audience might well have recognized that Paracelsus' sixteenth-century medicine held up no better to modern scientific scrutiny than many other arcane practices that had fallen into disuse. So the reader is left to judge who got the better bargain in that particular exchange.

The roots of medical orthodoxies have always been closely entwined with ideological and theological assumptions. For Roger to assign Indian lore comparable credibility to European medical knowledge would have offended the belief systems of those who aligned the explorations of Protestant Europe with God's will and revelation, and have cast suspicion even upon his most successful healing efforts. Indeed, as time passes, despite a growing reputation for medical skill, dark rumors circulate to the effect that Roger "had enlarged his medical attainments by joining in the incantations of the savage priests, who were universally acknowledged to be powerful enchanters, often performing seemingly miraculous cures by their skill in the black art." The same townspeople, "persons of such sober sense and practical observation that their opinions would have been valuable in other matters," observe the change in Roger (which we, dear readers, have ample reason to attribute to his obsession with revenge) and presume that it comes from satanic practices. They spread abroad the "vulgar idea" that "the fire in his laboratory had been brought from the lower regions, and was fed with infernal fuel."

Suspicion of this kind, if not quite so unveiled, continues, of course, to be levied at various "alternative" approaches to medicine as well as at religious heterodoxies, especially by certain Christians for whom anything derived from non-Christian teachings or "new age" notions of spirituality and health is, by definition, anathema. Hawthorne's reclamation of a gospel word of inclusiveness might be just as unsettling to some readers of our generation as to those of his own. Where the exclusive dimension of Christ's message is made the measure of the church's integrity, and even of "Christian culture," inclusivity may be perceived as a kind of spiritual erosion. And the analogy, if not alignment, between medical and theological orthodoxy continues behind the closed doors of conferences to which the unorthodox need not apply and funding institutions whose research and development money is not accessible to purveyors of herbs and energy therapies.

So the medically unorthodox join the ranks of "dissenters" whose fate in American history and literature has been so remarkably two-sided. They are both heroes and scapegoats—the Captain Ahabs and Huck Finns and Kerouacs who fly against the prevailing winds of doctrine, but whose own courses seem so ill-fated, or at least indeterminate. Religious dissenters, of course, make up the starring cast of early settlers in the Northeast, but one dissenting group in particular proved to be very hard on others. Persecuted as they were, the most stringent of the separatists in New England became in their turn persecutors. And the irony of this post-Reformation turnabout was not lost upon Hawthorne, who found, 200 years later, that the spirit of exclusivity continued to inform a church he found both repellant and compelling enough to merit the close and sometimes anguished attention he gives it, especially in this, his finest work.

Part of that anguish is certainly attributable to his own delicate sense of guilt by inheritance and association with the "first ancestor"—the witch-trial judge, John Hathorne—who, he confesses in "The Custom House," "was present to my boyish imagination as far back as I can remember" and who "still haunts me." His description of this spectral figure reads like a character treatment for the magistrates in Hester Prynne's Boston:

He was a soldier, legislator, judge; he was a ruler in the Church; he had all the Puritanic traits, both good and evil. He was likewise a bitter persecutor; as witness the Quakers, who have remembered him in their histories, and relate an incident of his hard severity towards a woman of their sect, which will last longer, it is to be feared, than any record of his better deeds, although these were many.

The "Puritanic traits" in question, "both good and evil," were apparently not confined to attitudes acquired by early and vigorous indoctrination, but, more mysteriously, transmitted by blood, culture, and the "atmosphere" that can become poisonous with human evil. One of the most poignant paragraphs in "The Custom House" frames the ensuing narrative as a confession and an act of penance for the rigid, exclusionary and punitive practices that marked the writer's social identity. Writing still of that early ancestor, he muses,

His son, too, inherited the persecuting spirit, and made himself so conspicuous in the martyrdom of the witches, that their blood may fairly be said to have left a stain upon him. So deep a stain, indeed, that his dry old bones, in the Charter-street burial-ground, must still retain it, if they have not crumbled utterly to dust! I know not whether these ancestors of mine bethought themselves to repent, and ask pardon of Heaven for their cruelties; or whether they are now groaning under the heavy consequences of them in another state of being. At all events, I, the present writer, as their representative, hereby take shame upon myself for their sakes, and pray that any curse incurred by them—as I have heard, and as the dreary and unprosperous condition of the race, for many a long year back, would argue to exist—may be now and henceforth removed.

What is made explicit in this passage, and is implicit in every chapter of the ensuing story, is the conviction that the worst crime of these harsh forebears is their judgment of those they deemed outsiders, and the right they abrogated to themselves not only to judge and convict, but to punish cruelly and unusually any they deemed heretics. And that crime is extended and exacerbated in the legacy of self-righteous cruelty passed on to children who played at "scourging Quakers; or taking scalps in a sham fight with the Indians, or scaring one another with freaks of imitative witchcraft." Taking to their own extreme a convenient misreading of "he that is not with me is against me" that has legitimated so much enmity and warfare, the early Puritans of Hawthorne's historical imagination failed to reckon with the many gentler and more open-ended gospel messages of tolerance, inclusion, and humility that leaves all judgment to the only one in a position to judge.

In Hester's story, and in Arthur's, Hawthorne articulates the spiritual and psychological consequences of the religious exclusion that he seems also to have seen as a dangerous fault line in American political life. Their respective stories offer what might be called "parables" of Christian punishment—one about those who live in exile from an unforgiving church, the other about those who stay on uneasy and disingenuous terms.

Arthur's of course, seems at face value not to be a story of exclusion, but of life at the epicenter of a history and hierarchy that not only fully authorize him as pastor and scholar, but that keep him safe from exposure and shame to which he appears so vulnerable. Yet Arthur's tormented conscience isolates him from the very people who follow and revere him. His self-imposed excommunication keeps him in a position of radical cognitive dissonance. Unable to claim the mercy he must preach, caught in the legalism of a church whose faith and whose God he loves, Arthur finds himself in a tragic situation no doubt replicated in many who have struggled to reconcile their faith in God and in Christ with a church that seems in so many ways to betray that faith. Standing in the pulpit in which he nevertheless locates his calling, he speaks powerfully and persuasively, his words echoing from the depths of a deep pit of self-accusation. In fact, his sermons seem, over years of debilitating struggle with unconfessed guilt, to grow steadily more eloquent, stirring, and efficacious, the guilt itself serving as something like a refining fire. On the morning after the strange and unnerving nighttime rendezvous on the scaffold with Hester and Pearl, who with him witness the appearance of a "great red letter in the sky—the letter A," he preaches

> a discourse which was held to be the richest and most power-
> ful, and the most replete with heavenly influences, that had ever
> proceeded from his lips. Souls, it is said, more souls than one,
> were brought to the truth by the efficacy of that sermon, and
> vowed within themselves to cherish a holy gratitude towards Mr.
> Dimmesdale throughout the long hereafter.

What better evidence might there be that the one who is not against the merciful and forgiving Christ is for him? Arthur's shame, a disease that finally kills him, does not, apparently, impede the power of a Spirit that uses him, as so many reluctant and wayward prophets have been used, to be a sharp and shining instrument of grace. A more skeptical reading might suggest that the eloquence itself provides a veil of deceit, but the narrative offers ample evidence that Arthur's own faith is authentic, and his longing for release not only from guilt but from sin, sincere. His is not the only flesh, after all, that has been chronically and tragically weak where the spirit was willing, nor is he the only outsider to find spiritual food in the "wilderness."

Hester's predicament, as she lives out her neighborly exile from the community that both punishes and depends on her, seems nearly opposite to his. "Strong with a woman's strength," Hester bears her burdens with a determination almost as unfathomable as Roger's obsession or Arthur's guilt. Living as an actual outsider, though like Arthur she conducts herself publicly according to her assigned roles both as penitent and Puritan matron, hers is arguably the greater task: to work out her salvation without the protection of institutional guidance, sacraments, sermons, or solace. The narrator takes stock of her relationship to the church in a memorably intimate and sobering portrait of a woman schooled by exile:

> She had wandered, without rule or guidance, in a moral wilderness, as vast, as intricate, and shadowy as the untamed forest. . . . Her intellect and heart had their home, as it were, in desert places, where she roamed as freely as the wild Indian in his woods. For years past she had looked from this estranged point of view at human institutions, and whatever priests or legislators had established; criticising all with hardly more reverence than the Indian would feel for the clerical band, the judicial robe, the pillory, the gallows, the fireside, or the church. The tendency of her fate and fortunes had been to set her free.

But if Hester's exclusion "sets her free," it also condemns her in that freedom to a lonely and uncertain path of spiritual invention. No longer able to rest safe in the arms of "mother church," or secure as a sheep in the fold, or to be led by the "kindly light" that should have shone from this city on a hill, and unable like the Psalmist to "love the law" that has been so misused against her, she survives by embracing her exclusion and accepting it ultimately as a call to a new kind of spiritual leadership.

Hawthorne's love of paradox comes to a high pitch in representing her religious and spiritual freedom as simultaneously a condemnation and a liberation. The way of the wanderer, outside the human institutions meant for our nurture and safety, is perilous. But the perilous way is also the way of the hero. In Hester we surely have one of the most lasting images of peculiarly American heroism. And to cast a woman in that role was certainly a thrust to the heart of one of the church's most troubling positions, at least those churches that took a strict constructionist attitude toward Paul's teaching that women should be silent, not teach, and certainly not preach, though they might minister in many other efficacious ways. At the end of the story, she is an outsider not because of the brand on her bosom—which has long since ceased to serve as a mark of shame—but because she gathers women around her and teaches them. She has become the wise woman who claims her own authority—a strong and promising figure, and one some members of the community can accredit, but one who also leans uncomfortably close to the darkly forested margin where "witches" were said to dwell.

"Witches," along with Indians and dissenters, were a class of outcasts for whom Hawthorne had, as we know, particular reason to be concerned. His great-grandfather's participation in the infamous Salem witch trials plagued his imagination, as one might be similarly troubled by the knowledge that an ancestor had been a notoriously cruel slave trader. Moreover, his critical view of church history, especially of its record of pharisaism, legalism, abuse of power, and suppression of women and other vulnerable populations, would have led him directly to speculate about the causes and effects of the more widespread European witch hunts of the fourteenth and fifteenth centuries. Though he was clearly fascinated with the mysterious energies and powers of nature that affect human health and behavior, and though his fancy led him (along with Poe and other Romantics) to muse about paranormal, "preternatural," events, his interest in them seems to have been rather more sociological and psychological than theological: he seemed less concerned with the dangers of occult practices than with the dangers of those whose politics, both ecclesial and secular, focused upon their eradication. Taking up his role as judicious historian, the narrator remarks on the Puritan culture of seventeenth-century Boston,

> Nothing was more common, in those days, than to interpret all meteoric appearances, and other natural phenomena that occurred with less regularity than the rise and set of sun and moon, as so many revelations from a supernatural source. Thus, a blazing spear, a sword of flame, a bow, or a sheaf of arrows seen in the midnight sky, prefigured Indian warfare.

Quaint as such readings of nature might seem, the implication becomes clear that such habits of mind, especially the compulsion to align natural "signs" with biblical prophecies, were dubious and dangerous practices that almost inevitably led to the spread of fear and violence.

Similarly, the necromancers, mad scientists, apparitions, and witches who populate his stories serve to call attention not so much to a serious theology of the occult as to the historical fact that those roles tended to be assigned to individuals or groups who threatened the prevailing ortho-doxies and power structures of Christian communities. Mistress Hibbens, of course, offers a case in point. Introduced as "Governor Bellingham's bitter-tempered sister" and the widow of a magistrate of the town, she enters the story most conspicuously when, as Hester and Pearl leave the Governor's mansion after enduring examination as to Hester's fitness to keep her daughter, she leans from a chamber window and with a stage-whispered "Hist, hist!" invites Hester to join a "merry company in the forest" that night to meet "the Black Man." Our incessantly ironic narrator pauses in the midst of this little scene to observe that the "ill-omened physiognomy [of this "witch lady"] seemed to cast a shadow over the cheerful newness of the house." He reports, moreover, in a mere aside, that she was later executed as a witch.

The proximity of this little encounter to the highly charged confron-tation between Hester and the four men who represent the legal, ecclesial, and medical powers to which she is subject gives it pointed significance. She has endured the humiliation of having to insist that Arthur, whose secrets and reputation she has protected at great cost, speak on her behalf, since her own words bear no weight in that company. Her devoted care of her child has been summarily ignored and put to a patently inappropri-ate test in a catechism whose terms Pearl herself subverts with complex, childlike truth telling. She is caught in the currents of male power-trading that has made starkly apparent her utter vulnerability to their vested in-terests. So when Mistress Hibbens invites her to join what we infer to be a witches' coven, Hester finds herself suddenly and strongly tempted:

> I must tarry at home, and keep watch over my little Pearl. Had they taken her from me, I would willingly have gone with thee into the forest, and signed my name in the Black Man's book too, and that with mine own blood!

Her response raises a core question in this tale that so insistently questions the terms on which we consign people and their acts to fixed categories of good and evil. How often, in other words, is "evil" a symptom of desperation born in a context of oppression?

Not to be overlooked in Hawthorne's recreation of the discourse of witchcraft is the term "Black Man" to designate the devil. Written for an audience sure to be densely populated with abolitionists, as the controversy over returning escaped slaves heated up and the Underground Railroad ran straight through his neighbors' houses in western Massachusetts, the story alludes with painful irony to the plight of a population much larger than, and analogous to, the hapless women of Salem in 1692. A whole history of bigotry is encapsulated in the association of "blackness" with sin and Satan. And the idea of white women drawn into the "wild" to meet a black man surely triggered layers of nonrational fear even in the more egalitarian-minded of Hawthorne's contemporaries. Fear of miscegenation had accounted for a good many death-dealing policies and practices by the time this story was crafted in a peaceful little New England town.

That history comes to seem particularly tragic where Hester's plight is reflected in Pearl's behavior. The question, introduced obliquely but repeatedly in the story, of how the sins of the parents are, in fact, visited upon the children receives one answer when we see Pearl as a victim of persecution, trained by exclusion and excoriation to her own brand of vigorous resistance. When the Puritan children mocked and attacked her,

> Pearl would grow positively terrible in her puny wrath, snatching
> up stones to fling at them, with shrill, incoherent exclamations,
> that made her mother tremble, because they had so much the
> sound of a witch's anathemas in some unknown tongue.

Several terms in this portrait deserve our attention. Pearl's wrath is "puny"; we are reminded in that single word that she is a child, powerless and weak. Her strategies of self-protection come not from a position of power, but of abject weakness and congenital starvation of the nourishment community provides. The casting of stones, of course, though the other children began it, ironically evokes Jesus' injunction, "Let him who is without sin among you cast the first stone," but also suggests how violence breeds violence and how logically the powerless are led to resort to the very forms violence from which they have suffered. Perhaps most interesting is the matter of language. In a book closely focused on the power of the word, of letters, of the letter of the law, and of public discourse, we cannot help but notice here again an allusion to the decisive effect of language not only as a bearer of meaning, but as a distinguishing feature of character and class.

Pearl's language is "shrill," "incoherent," and incomprehensible, even to her mother. It seems both alien and indigenous to this child who has no home in the discourse of the community around her. Though she appears again and again as a truth teller in her confrontations with the adults who govern her world, she tells her truths "slant." She articulates her sharp intuitions as questions designed to elicit confession rather than levy accusation. In the forest, when her mother meets the minister and removes her letter for the first time, she resorts to the wail of an inarticulate small child, very like that of an animal (or of Arthur, whose involuntary shrieks in the anguish of his midnight vigil are registered only in others' dreams where it was taken for "the noise of witches . . . as they rode with Satan through the air"), to protest the disruption of the one anchor—a letter— that offers her a sense of home. So the idea suggested in this passage that her language resembles "a witch's anathema" raises the larger question of how secret and privileged language—speaking in tongues, spells, incantations, or antique formulae—empowers and sets apart populations who have no other access to power.

As a form of self-empowerment, Pearl's "witchcraft" seems not altogether ominous. In this small child, access to the world of natural energies, spirits, even elves and fairies, or, more to the point, the power of imagination and spiritual openness, lead to the transformation and animation of simple things so characteristic of unimpeded childlike play. Her magic is the magic of a mind open to possibility: "The unlikeliest materials—a stick, a bunch of rags, a flower—were the puppets of Pearl's witchcraft, and, without undergoing any outward change, became spiritually adapted to whatever drama occupied the stage of her inner world." The same might be said of any child deeply absorbed in imaginative play. To call such engagement "witchcraft" leads us to wonder what, in fact, it is that we call witchcraft. The ancient associations between artistic creativity, poetic sensibility, special sensitivities and magic, madness, or outlawry suggest that what remains unconfirmed to community standards, those who speak from the margins and offer alternative points of view to the dominant orthodoxies, will, if they cannot be silenced, be controlled by labeling and exclusion. In women, especially, introspection, imagination, intelligence, and initiative posed direct threats to patriarchy, and it was an easy step from identifying that threat to labeling it witchcraft, thereby marshalling the forces of church and state against it.

Even Arthur, gentle as he attempts to be with Pearl in the course of their infrequent and painful encounters, fears in her wrath some uncontrollable force that he associates with the "fiends and night-hags" who consort with the "witch-lady," Mistress Hibbens. Witnessing Pearl's childish tantrum in the forest, occasioned by her mother's removing the scarlet letter, he begs Hester to silence her: "Save it were the cankered wrath of an old witch like Mistress Hibbens," he explains, "I know nothing that I would not sooner encounter than this passion in a child. In Pearl's young beauty as in the wrinkled witch, it has a preternatural effect. Pacify her if thou lovest me!"

To most parents of young children, this plea has its comic side. Who has not known the desperate end-of-the-rope moments when all attempts to quiet a hysterical child fail? But in Arthur's haste to describe Pearl's anger as "preternatural," and to associate it with the "cankered wrath" of an old witch, we see the seeds of a sick defense of his own forms of power that fails utterly to amuse. Moreover, to ask Hester to silence her daughter as proof of her love for him puts her once again in a place of choosing between, on the one hand, a natural tie with its nuanced and intuitive modes of understanding, and socially imposed structures of male control. The legitimacy of childhood, motherhood, womanhood, the wild, and even the movement of the Spirit that "blows where it listeth" are at stake in this contest.

Witches, in any event, are women who know things. They know too much, and they know in ways that do not submit to the governance of church, state, or academy. As Pearl knows more than she can say, Mistress Hibbens knows more than she will say; both resort to indirection to tell what they know.

The old woman, encountering Arthur after his troubling tryst with Hester in the forest, invites him to meet her there again, to meet the prince of darkness with whom he is so surely connected. Arthur insists his errand into the wilderness was "to greet that pious friend of mine, the Apostle Eliot, and rejoice with him over the many precious souls he hath won from heathendom!" The old woman's response cuts right through his falsehood: "You carry it off like an old hand!"

As in so many biblical stories, it is the sinners who know themselves for what they are. Neither Roger nor Mistress Hibbens nor Hester nor Pearl nor the tortured Arthur harbors illusions about their own righteousness—those appear to be the province of the people in power. It is the latter who presume to condemn others—dissenters, Indians, and uppity women—to exonerate themselves. Their exclusionary theology, drawing heavily on the principle that those not for us are against us, neglects at great cost the complementary scriptural dictum: those not against us are for us. Insisting on the complementary importance of the latter teaching, Hawthorne's homiletic imagination leaves us once again musing on paradox, without which, it appears, the truth, which is always multidimensional, cannot be adequately told.

-8-

Sick and in Prison

I was sick and ye visited me:
I was in prison and ye came unto me.

MATTHEW 25:36

To readers who remember Roger Chillingworth as a conniving, disingenuous, vindictive meddler, I'd like to commend a rereading of the moving scene in chapter 4 where he visits Hester in prison. Despite the downward spiral of revenge that transforms him into the shriveled, satanic figure he becomes in the end, one cannot pass final judgment on him without recalling that he is apparently the only one in town to visit Hester in prison, and there to perform several works of conditional, but timely mercy. Indeed, he himself is lodged in the same prison, pending ransom negotiations with the Indians who have released him, and so he shares Hester's bleak temporary housing—an image at least worth considering in terms of what it might mean to be in a position to minister to the outcast.

At the time of his visit, Hester has reached the end of her rope. She has stood exposed on the scaffold all day, holding her child who is

113

now wailing, seeming (our narrator theorizes) to have drunk in with her mother's milk "all the turmoil, the anguish and despair, which pervaded the mother's system." There might be simpler explanations for a baby's wailing, but Hawthorne takes a high view of what Montessori called children's "absorbent minds." They know more than we think they do and communicate in ways we tend to forget once we are acculturated to the proprieties of rational discourse. Nevertheless, whatever elevated view one might take of a baby's fussy behavior, anyone who has held one in the course of a sleepless night knows how it can fray the nerves and drive even the most devoted parent to distraction. When Roger is ushered into Hester's cell, Pearl is writhing in "convulsions of pain," and her mother is reduced to "a state of nervous excitement that demanded constant watchfulness, lest she should perpetrate violence on herself, or do some half-frenzied mischief to the poor babe." The jailer has called Roger in hope that as a physician he might be able to "quell her insubordination."

The fact that he has learned to view as insubordination such manifestations of pain and desperation should not be lost on us. A whole history of punitive justice lies in that well-chosen word. Like so many prisoners before and since, Hester suffers for a crime committed, as Roger generously recognizes, in circumstances that left her vulnerable to temptation beyond what she could bear. And the fact that the jailer calls a physician rather than a guard in this instance indicates at least some honest and healthy confusion on his part about whether to treat the prisoner as perpetrator or patient. His own sympathy is conspicuously limited; handing her over to Roger, he offers a grim diagnosis: "Verily, the woman hath been like a possessed one; and there lacks little that I should take in hand, to drive Satan out of her with stripes." Still, with a grudging mercy, he gives medicine a try.

Here, as throughout the story, sin and sickness appear to be inextricably intertwined, reinforcing the juxtaposition of the two in Jesus' own formula: "Sick and in prison and ye visited me not." When on the opening page our narrator remarks that among the first buildings of a new colony must be a prison and a burial ground, he reminds us that our common condition leads us to one or both. It therefore behooves us, it seems, not to regard either as alien territory; they image forth truths about ourselves we can't afford to forget. But the relationship of sin or crime to sickness and death was, and remains, vexed. Even in the biblical texts the clear link between Adam's sin and humankind's mortality is rendered more complicated by the deaths of innocents, and by Jesus' own assertion that the disability of a man is not, in fact, a direct consequence of his own or his parents' sins (John 9:1–3). Public policy still reflects some uncertainty as to what behaviors to criminalize and what to treat as illness—addictions, compulsions, and sundry sociopathologies being cases in point. By most standards, even in 1850, Hester's case would hardly merit particularly harsh judgment, though the women of the town, as we have seen, inflicted their worst. Roger and the jailer both act, if not in pure compassion, at least in recognition of a need that matters more than administration of punishment. Unlikely agents of mercy though they are, there they are, standing at Hester's door, more willing than most to address her predicament.

The narrator's evident sympathy with that predicament invites ours as well: he calls our attention to the "dismal" apartment, to the "moral agony" Hester has borne, and her "depressed" state, eliciting our sympathies with language that emphasizes suffering over sin. Then his report of their "interview" recedes to a respectful distance as we witness the curious dialogue between the estranged husband and wife, now bound by a new set of circumstances to a new kind of dependence upon each other. He gives us at the outset every reason to trust that there is kindness in Roger's motives for visiting the prisoner: the fact that "his first care was given to the child," that he "examined the infant carefully," and that he offers an effective healing "draught" to Hester for the baby lay a foundation of credibility against which we must measure his mixed motives. Roger's response to Hester's suspicion that he may have come with poison seems the healthy indignation of a reasonable man: "What should ail me to harm this misbegotten and miserable babe? The medicine is potent for good and, were it my child—yea, mine own, as well as thine! I could do no better for it." Both the medicine he gives the child and the medicine he then gives the mother bring swift comfort.

Roger, we later learn, is driven by an ultimately tragic urge toward revenge. But in this early chapter he appears not as a man hell-bent on a vendetta, but as a learned physician who has lived among Indians who are generally feared and suspected by their white neighbors, and has learned from them. Having re-entered the society of European colonists, he carries out a Christ-like mission of identifying with and ministering to the outcast. Indeed, it is his capacity to extend such compassion that makes his darker motives the more truly tragic, for we are led in scenes like this one to imagine a capacity for great goodness in him.

A bit of Roger's later history is pertinent to the writer's purposes—here again, to complicate our sympathies and move us beyond easy moral judgments. In both Roger's story and Hester's, Hawthorne shows how good can come out of evil and vice versa. Acknowledging that paradox, which has strong biblical underpinnings, we must also come again to see that we are not in a position to judge either state with certainty: we cannot assume we know how to reckon the moral accounts of "evil" men who perform unexpected acts of kindness or of "good" ones who see in their most sober self-examinations what T. S. Eliot identified as "things ill done, and done to others' harm / which once you took for exercise of virtue."[1] The story of Roger's earlier life is remarkable only as a record of extraordinary intellectual appetite and what might seem commendable, healthy, detached curiosity about the world of the sort one hopes for in a responsible scientist. He had consistently been "calm in temperament, kindly, though not of warm affections, but ever, and in all his relations with the world, a pure and upright man." More reasonable than might be expected, upon learning of his wife's infidelity, and suspecting the minister, he is still restrained by something more than self-serving cunning:

> He had begun an investigation, as he imagined, with the severe and equal integrity of a judge, desirous only of truth, even as if the question involved no more than the air-drawn lines and figures of a geometrical problem, instead of human passions, and wrongs inflicted on himself. But, as he proceeded, a terrible fascination, a kind of fierce, though still calm, necessity, seized the old man within its grip, and never set him free again until he had done all its bidding.

What later appears to be a diabolical lust for vengeance began, it seems, in a reasonable desire for justice. Moreover, the degeneration of Roger's motives is described here not as a matter of ill will so much as a sickness in its own right, or at least a state of mind and heart for which he may not be entirely responsible. Like any other addiction, it takes hold of him, as it were, from the outside, and makes him its slave. Thus the question of his culpability is vexed at the outset.

---

1. Eliot, *Four Quartets*, 54.

Curiously, as Roger grows more vindictive, he sounds more like the pious men whose company he has taken to keeping. He consorts with Governor Bellingham and Reverend Wilson as well as with Arthur, taking his place among the "worthies" of the town, and his hortatory encounter with Arthur in his sickroom seems, ironically, most aggressive where he assumes most explicitly the admonitory tone of those elders: "Would thou have me to believe, O wise and pious friend," he asks Arthur rhetorically, "that a false show can be better—can be more for God's glory, or man' welfare—than God's own truth? Trust me, such men deceive themselves!" Such language strikes a false note, especially contrasted with some of Roger's harsh but straightforward exchanges with Hester, who shares with him a commitment to unvarnished truth, having nothing to lose in telling it to him. The rude implication seems to be that Roger's cunning and cruelty are rooted more in his appropriation of the punitive ethic and discourse of this brand of Puritan than in his own desire to ferret out the truth.

Faust-like, as many a reader has pointed out, Roger wants knowledge. It is a dangerous desire, if separated from the motive of love. That separation widens as he pursues the truth about Arthur:

> He . . . dug into the poor clergyman's heart, like a miner searching for gold; or, rather, like a sexton delving into a grave, possibly in quest of a jewel that had been buried on the dead man's bosom, but likely to find nothing save mortality and corruption. Alas, for his own soul, if these were what he sought!

Yet the narrator leaves open the possibility that these proofs of Arthur's spiritual decay were not all Roger sought. Even in his obsession, Roger is driven by an interest we might be quick to commend in a research scientist. Musing aloud on one of his visits to Arthur's sick room, Roger expostulates on the theory that physical diseases of the sort he sees in Arthur often have a spiritual dimension. Circumspectly, he suggests that if Arthur wants to be cured, he might do well to disclose any spiritual distresses that might be relevant to his physical ailment. Arthur, however, immediately and vigorously refuses the implied invitation, insisting (as many still might) that a physician's proper sphere is care of the body, not the soul. But his rejection doesn't put Roger off. Rather he pursues his reflections a step further, "going on, in an unaltered tone, without heeding the interruption, but standing up and confronting the emaciated and white-cheeked minister, with his low, dark, and misshapen figure." The dramatic effect of one damaged body facing the other in this moment of reflection on what the body reveals is not to be overlooked, suggesting as it does a strong similarity between physician and patient. Both are stricken, in both there seems to be an accord between their physical infirmities and their spiritual conditions.

What follows this little approach-and-avoidance conversation throws into question the notion that Roger is obsessed with vengeance: Roger simply assents to the minister's terms and "went on with his medical supervision of the minister; doing his best for him, in all good faith, but always quitting the patient's apartment, at the close of the professional interview, with a mysterious and puzzled smile upon his lips." Finding Arthur's a "rare case," he mutters to himself, in tones our lurking narrator can no doubt barely catch from behind whatever nearby tree he has been hovering, "I must needs look deeper into it. A strange sympathy betwixt soul and body! Were it only for the art's sake, I must search this matter to the bottom." Arguably, his dedication to the "art" of medicine mitigates his darker intentions. His fascination with the nature of the whole person bespeaks a large and inclusive understanding of what medicine might rightly embrace.

Those intentions are unsettlingly apparent in a later encounter when, finding Arthur asleep, the physician uncovers his chest and finds something (A mark? A brand? We are left to speculate) that confirms his theory. He turns away with "a wild look of wonder, joy, and horror," so exultant that he "threw up his arms towards the ceiling and stamped his foot upon the floor!" The narrator pointedly—not to say heavy-handedly—compares his comportment in this gleeful moment of discovery to what Satan's must be "when a precious soul is lost to heaven, and won into his kingdom," casting Roger's motives in the worst possible light. Yet immediately the narrator strikes a redemptive note: "But what distinguished the physician's ecstasy from Satan's was the trait of wonder in it!" Whatever Roger saw taught him something about the connection of body and spirit that he longed to understand. Surely understanding that relationship is a worthy motive. It was one that underlay much of Hawthorne's own speculations, and his fellow Transcendentalists'.

Whatever undermined Roger's "care" of Arthur, the story also reminds us repeatedly of the lively relationship between curiosity and compassion, and of the goodness of the thirst for knowledge that fosters true humility—such humility, for instance, as would have been required to enter into the alien culture of native peoples and learn from them, and bring that learning into the sickrooms of European immigrants entrenched in their own limited medical culture. Even in his most intimate invasion of Arthur's privacy, we may discern an element of kindness fueled by authentic interest that offsets the extravagant demonic imagery that lures us into the too-easy judgments the writer always ultimately undermines.

Among the various kindnesses to be reckoned to Roger's account is the fact of his final generosity toward Pearl, the child of his wife's adultery. Leaving her all his money, he frees her to claim a life where illegitimacy won't foreclose all opportunity. He treats her, in effect, as his own child. He watches her closely, makes astute observations about her nature, keeps a respectful distance from her, but finally bestows upon her the one recognition that gives her what her father couldn't and her mother can't: the means to make a place for herself in a world beyond the exclusionary confines of a community that does not know how to make a place for her, since the very terms of her birth have put her outside the law. Roger's is an act of grace— or can at least be seen as one—that indicts their narrow understanding and application of the law. It comes from a dubious source, but works to a life-giving end, leaving us once again with the bemusing reminder that we cannot separate wheat from tares or good from evil without destroying something in the place where the sword of judgment falls.

Like Roger, Hester visits the sick. Throughout her years of "ignominy," she maintains her isolation from society except where opportunities for service allow her entry. Among the sick and dying she finds a venue for her skills, honed by her own training in anguish and loss. She is comfortable as few others are with darkness and sorrow. Reviewing the course of her life in the wake of the scaffold, the narrator pays sustained and generous tribute to her many works of mercy:

> . . . she was quick to acknowledge her sisterhood with the race of man whenever benefits were to be conferred. None so ready as she to give of her little substance to every demand of poverty, even though the bitter-hearted pauper threw back a gibe in requital of the food brought regularly to his door, or the garments wrought for him by the fingers that could have embroidered a monarch's robe. None so self-devoted as Hester when pestilence stalked through the town.

This representation of Hester's saintly devotion to townspeople is imbedded in the same chapter ("Another View of Hester") that recounts her
darkest, bitterest hours, her attraction to witches' covens, her temptation
to suicide. As in Roger's story, but with a more redemptive trajectory,
good and evil mingle in odd and uncomfortable ways. It is impossible, if
one accepts the narrator's inside information, to consider either of these
troubled healers without accepting considerable moral ambiguity. Their
healing powers, it is clearly suggested, are a direct result of their having
ventured into the "wilderness," both literal and moral, and having learned
there something that prepared and empowered them for service. Though
the information we receive about Roger emphasizes his singular obsession
with exposing Arthur's paternity, we also learn that he becomes, over time,
a trusted and successful physician in the town, whose knowledge of the
healing properties of plants has brought benefit to many. Similarly Hester
has allowed herself to be "taught" by the instrument of her exclusion and
the resourcefulness required to survive it. Consequently, they find a common calling in visiting the sick. "In all seasons of calamity" we are told,
Hester, an "outcast of society . . . found her place." Lest we underestimate
the social importance of this vocation, the narrator continues warmly,

> She came, not as a guest, but as a rightful inmate, into the house-
> hold that was darkened by trouble, as if its gloomy twilight were
> a medium in which she was entitled to hold intercourse with her
> fellow-creature. Elsewhere the token of sin, [the embroidered let-
> ter] was the taper of the sick chamber . . . In such emergencies
> Hester's nature showed itself warm and rich—a well-spring of hu-
> man tenderness, unfailing to every real demand, and inexhaust-
> ible by the largest. Her breast, with its badge of shame, was but the
> softer pillow for the head that needed one. She was self-ordained
> a Sister of Mercy, or, we may rather say, the world's heavy hand
> had so ordained her, when neither the world nor she looked for-
> ward to this result . . . It was only the darkened house that could
> contain her.

Nowhere in the story are we more clearly encouraged to see sin and its
consequences as a form of suffering that can open the heart and dissolve
the pretenses that prevent selfless service. The biblical message that those
who receive mercy are equipped to become agents of mercy is clearly il-
lustrated in Hester's powerful ministry even to those who won't receive
her. Both she and Roger, having accepted the risk and the forfeitures of
outsider status, have access to others' vulnerabilities that those in elevated

positions of political and ecclesial authority do not. Neither Arthur nor Governor Bellingham nor old Reverend Wilson, though they enjoy the respect of the townspeople, is free to enter their compatriots' lives through the back door, so to speak. They are protected by rank and ceremony from the physical and spiritual squalor in which people find themselves in greatest need. By contrast, Hester is "self-ordained," and utterly vulnerable. Her vocation and spiritual aptitude come, perhaps like that of the woman at the well who was made an unlikely evangelist, from a source no neighbors can account for by their limited theology.

Just as Jesus answered the Pharisees' question, "Who is my neighbor?" with a story about a member of an enemy tribe who becomes an agent of extravagant mercy, our narrator holds up two characters conspicuously marked by waywardness as the ones who "hear the word of the Lord and do it." Even in her repentance, Hester cannot be unambiguously described as a woman of great faith; rather, she is a woman who wrestles with serious temptation and doubt even as she accepts her imposed penance and exceeds its requirements. Moreover, that wrestling may be precisely what keeps her heart open toward others' secret sorrows and shames as well as their suffering.

Neither Hester's nor Roger's acts of mercy issue from anything we might recognize as wholehearted repentance and changing of ways. They are aware of their own mixed motives and the stirrings of anger and bitterness that sometimes overcome all worthier motives. Indeed, Roger is not only unrepentant, but more deeply steeped in revenge as the story goes on. So we may be inclined to discount his original kindness as the "lurid" fire of his vengeance begins to consume whatever good will was in him. Yet even in the midst of his vengeful pursuit of Arthur, he shows kindness toward the child, a certain graciousness toward Hester, and benevolence toward the people of the town. Hester is oddly comfortable in conversation with him, though at odds; they speak as equals. Pearl plays untroubled in his presence, and his observations of her are penetrating and accurate.

So we are led to ask ourselves at the end of this story as Jesus does at the end of his, "Which of these acted as a neighbor?" The disciples reply, "He that shewed mercy . . ." (Luke 10:36–37). We are invited, as they were, to acknowledge that the ones who in "hearing the word of the Lord and doing it" earn divine blessing may often be the very ones the more self-satisfied regard from a safe distance with condescension or scorn. They themselves may be surprised. Jesus' words recorded in Matthew's Gospel indicate that many of those welcomed as faithful servants will not, themselves, recognize their own membership in the kingdom, but rather will ask, puzzled, "When saw we thee a stranger, and took thee in? or naked, and clothed thee? Or when saw we thee sick, or in prison, and came unto thee?" Jesus' answer, simple and profound and utterly reliable as a measure of Christian charity, cuts through all the pharisaical casuistry that confuses the matter of how best to serve God: "Inasmuch as ye have done it unto one of the least of these my brethren, ye have done it unto me" (Matt 25:38–40).

It is easier to exonerate Hester at the end of the story than Roger. But both have served others in perhaps the only way humans can serve—with murky intentions, mixed motives, doubts, resentments, and radical uncertainties. Both challenge us to take a wider view of what may be honored and accepted as coming from the hand of God in our midst. In her memorable rereading of the parable of the Good Samaritan, Margaret Mohrmann points out that one of the questions the story pointedly raises for those to whom it is told—people who would find the very touch of a Samaritan repugnant—is this: "From whom are you willing to accept help?" More commonly read as a challenge to help those with whom we are not inclined to identify, she turns the story to another angle:

> The answer Jesus gives to the question—"Who is my neighbor? Who is this person I am required to love even as I love myself?"— is that my neighbor is the Samaritan, my neighbor is the one who shows me mercy. I am not the Samaritan; I am the one who needs the Samaritan . . . This is not a pleasant picture. How can I be the helpless, damaged person lying by the side of the road? I am the doctor, I am the minister, I am the healer. I bind up wounds; I do not have them, at least not any wounds that I shall allow to be tended by any Samaritan who comes down the road and happens to find me.[2]

The unsettling conclusion to this reading is this: those of us safely ensconced in communities where others are comfortably like us, law-abiding, churchgoing, "good" people, may have more need than we realize of the outcasts, even the outlaws who just possibly come among us as instruments of a grace that is truly, disturbingly, and in the most literal sense, amazing.

---

2. Mohrmann, *Medicine as Ministry*, 42–43.

-9-

A Great Price

The kingdom of heaven is like unto a merchant man
. . . who, when he had found one pearl of great price,
went and sold all that he had, and bought it.

MATTHEW 13:45–6

UNTIL THE FINAL CHAPTER of *The Scarlet Letter,* Hester never appears without Pearl nearby. From the opening scene at the scaffold where she stands holding her baby in her arms like an "image of the Divine Maternity" to the climactic moment of Dimmesdale's confession and death where she holds him like the Virgin of the Pietà, Pearl is there as witness, participant, and defining circumstance of her mother's life. Had little Pearl never "come to her from the spiritual world," the narrator suggests, the course of Hester's life might have been "far otherwise." She might indeed have been another Anne Hutchinson—a prophetess and crusader. But because she is a mother, particularly because she is a single mother, her destiny does not work itself out in those public ways. "In the education of her child," the narrator explains, "the mother's enthusiasm had something to wreak itself upon." Pearl is Hester's mission, her means of self-expression, her mirror, her stumbling block, her "one treasure," a spur

123

to her speculations, a reminder of her disgrace, an incarnate philosophical problem, and a "providential" provision for Hester's own survival and ultimate growth into a woman of complex wisdom. As for many women, motherhood pervades every area of Hester's life, from her most intimate reflections upon her own identity to her most public social encounters.

Motherhood, however, is not only a natural condition, but a label that carries a large connotative load. It has been mythologized, ensconced in religious and legal definition, and infused with the values of patriarchy. In an essentially patriarchal culture, motherhood becomes a male-defined institution, both nurturing and self-defeating. Adrienne Rich has offered one perspective on this institution in examining her own experience of motherhood that echoes the experience represented with such insight by Hawthorne a century earlier:

> I realize that I was effectively alienated from my real body and my real spirit by the institution—not the fact—of motherhood. This institution—the foundation of human society as we know it—allowed me only certain views, certain expectations, whether embodied in the booklet in my obstetrician's waiting room, the novels I had read, my mother-in-law's approval, my memories of my own mother, the Sistine Madonna or she of the Michelangelo Pietà.[1]

Rich goes on to point out that the institution of motherhood is also a pervasive idea: "Motherhood—unmentioned in the histories of conquest and serfdom, wars and treaties, exploration and imperialism—has a history, it has an ideology, it is more fundamental than tribalism or nationalism."[2] Attempting, then, to live out the deeply personal relationship and psychic reality of motherhood, a woman is also compelled to bear the weight of a large social and historical burden, to work out some relationship to the institution and the myths of motherhood. The process can result in what Rich points out is a "dangerous schism between 'private' and 'public' life," in ambivalence, contradiction, and conflict.[3]

One of the ways patriarchal society has mythologized motherhood is to regard it as the primary female calling. The idea has been propounded in imagery and doctrine by Christian churches for centuries. As recently as 1972, Pope Paul VI asserted that "true women's liberation

---

1. Rich, *Of Woman Born*, 38–39.
2. Ibid., 34.
3. Ibid., 13.

does not lie in 'formalistic or materialistic equality with the other sex,' but in the recognition of that specific thing in the feminine personality—the vocation of a woman to become a mother."[4] On the basis of this and comparable authority, childbearing has been made into a measure of women's lives. Terms like "barren" or "childless" have been used to diminish other dimensions of women's identities and contributions. It's worth noting in this regard that no comparable terms apply to men who "fail" to become fathers.

Motherhood has provided not only a *raison d'etre*, but also a means of atonement for the "sin" of femaleness implicit in much of Christian thought. If women, as Tertullian claimed, are "Eves," transmitters of sin and "gateways of the devil,"[5] it is their motherhood that vindicates and atones for their sinful sexuality. As a mother a woman is a transmitter of life, of (patriarchal) culture, and of (patriarchal) values. She is an important functionary in a social system in which she has historically had little voice but which has been represented as the unfolding of a divine plan. In order to function properly within that system, the conditions and obligations of her motherhood have had to be carefully defined: legitimacy, in particular, confers honor, and the bearing of the father's name. The kinds of ostracism borne by "unwed mothers" (one does not hear of "unwed fathers") and illegitimate children such as Hester and Pearl provide an indicator of what legitimate maternity means in a patriarchy.

It is instructive to examine the strange, ambiguous relationship between Hester and "her little Pearl" as an emblem of motherhood and a schematic portrayal of its problems. Compounded by the extremities of her situation, Hester's plight is nevertheless poignantly typical.

In the governor's hall, when Hester is brought face to face with two magistrates who represent the only recognized legal and religious authority of the community, and who threaten ("kindly") to take her child away, Hester cannot count upon the security of recognized parental rights unless she exercises them in accordance with these men's convictions. She is in an impossible double bind. She is to raise Pearl as a believing, practicing member of a religious community that has axiomatically excluded her, given her no support or sustenance beyond a meager living and the right to walk the streets physically unmolested, albeit publicly humiliated.

4. Pope Paul VI, *The Pope Speaks*, 335.

5. Tertullian, *De Cultu Feminarum*, Section 1.1, Part 2.

She has been locked into a paradoxical role that gives her duties but no rights, penance but no forgiveness. The motherhood that would ordinarily exonerate her from the "original sin" of her womanhood loses its value because it is not carried out on the terms of the men who define the terms of procreation and family life. One need only consider the obverse of her situation to recognize a corresponding limitation placed upon women who operate within those confines: they, too, are bound—to a pattern of expectations that limit their options and define their duties. A mother is "safe"—occupied with a task that will effectively prevent her from meddling in the larger world and becoming a "prophetess" or a public leader or a threat to the male establishment. Her "confinement" stretches far beyond the day of her giving birth. Her task involves much more than bringing a child into the world, feeding and clothing it, and educating it to survive in society. She must be a mediator, instructor, intepreter, protector, provider, comforter, and example to her child. Besides this she is supposed to live up to a standard of motherhood dictated by religion, law, and custom.

Law solidifies this standard. Even out on the periphery where Hester lives, the motherhood myth is inescapable. Hester has no precedents, no language, no tradition to pass on to her daughter but those that have been her own stumbling block. Her only guidelines for being a mother come from the mother she had and the mothers around her—pious women living out their roles in obedience (or suppressed rebellion) to the men in authority over them. On the scaffold, Hester thinks of her own mother's face, "with the look of heedful and anxious love which it always wore in her remembrance, and which, even since her death, had so often laid the impediment of a gentle remonstrance in her daughter's pathway."

One manifestation of this kind of watchfulness (which surely has its beauty as a demonstration of love, however limiting a vision it imposed) was the custom practiced among some Puritan women of writing "legacies" for their unborn children, lest, dying in childbirth, they should leave their children motherless. One such legacy, written in 1624 by Elizabeth Jocelin, a Puritan colonist, offers a fairly representative picture of the obligations a dutiful mother felt toward her daughter:

> I desire her bringing up may be learning the Bible, as my sisters
> doe good housewifery, writing, and good workes: other learning
> a woman needs not, though I admire it in those whom God hath
> blest with discretion, yet I desired not much in my owne, having
> seene that sometimes women have greater portions of learning

than wisdome, which is of no better use to them than a maine saile
to a flye-boat, which runs it under water.[6]

In just such a conscientious manner Hester, the "daughter of a pious
home," attempts to do her duty by Pearl. She teaches her the catechism
from the standard texts. She assures her, "Thy Heavenly Father made
thee," though, the narrator observes, "she said it with a hesitation that did
not escape the acuteness of the child."

Hester no longer believes what she "should" believe or feels what she
"should" feel. The constant irony in her interaction with society renders
it impossible for her ever again to accept its standards as "natural," God-
given, or absolute. Since everything she does is a message to her daughter,
the overwhelming question for Hester is what to tell Pearl.

She first confronts this question in the negative: what not to tell her.
The narrator recounts several pregnant moments of intimacy between
Hester and Pearl when authentic communication from heart to heart
seems possible, but each time she backs down from the opportunity,
fearful both of and for her child. She begins her life as Pearl's mother by
hiding from her, covering "the fatal token" on her breast when the baby
reaches for it. "From that epoch," the narrator intones, "Hester had never
felt a moment's safety; not a moment's calm enjoyment of her." The last
luxury of privacy is denied Hester. Pearl is her public. The child's constant
presence at her side means constant exposure to the scrutinizing gaze of
someone who tries to read her truth in the scarlet letter on her bosom.
But to become "an open book" to the child would mean to expose her to
an extreme conflict of authority—to allow her to experience and understand somehow the polarity between her mother and the rest of society,
and Hester cannot bring herself to force such a crisis.

At the beginning of her book, *My Mother / My Self*, Nancy Friday
speaks of the effect upon a daughter of a mother's "hiding," recognizing
in her own experience a common cultural pattern:

> I have always lied to my mother. And she to me. How young was I
> when I learned her language, to call things by other names? Five,
> four—younger? Her denial of whatever she could not tell me, that
> her mother could not tell her, and about which society enjoined us
> both to keep silent, distorts our relationship still.[7]

6. Jocelin, *The Mother's Legacie*, 58.

7. Friday, *My Mother / My Self*, 1.

The very protectiveness that seeks to spare the child endangers the relationship meant to be most nourishing and secure.

There are times, however, in her loneliness, when Hester wonders
whether it might not be that Pearl could help her—whether indeed it
might not "be her errand to soothe away the sorrow that lay cold in her
mother's heart and converted it into a tomb." Yet even at such a moment,
when Pearl, holding her mother's hand in both her own, turns her face up-
ward and questions her searchingly, "What does the letter mean, mother?
—and why dost thou wear it?" Hester declines the challenge:

> "What shall I say?" thought Hester to herself.—"No! If this be the
> price of the child's sympathy, I cannot pay it."
> Then she spoke aloud.
> "Silly Pearl," said she, "what questions are these? There are many
> things in this world that a child must not ask about."

Her dilemma is another double bind. Either she must undercut all
she has taught Pearl about the world or she must jeopardize her intimacy
with her daughter by refusing to reveal herself and hiding behind a rebuke.
The problem drives her to an all-too-familiar kind of desperate solution:
"Hold thy tongue, naughty child! . . ." she cries out "with an asperity that
she had never permitted to herself before." "Do not tease me; else I shall
shut thee into the dark closet!"

Hester is Pearl's window onto the world—at least onto the world of
society—yet she cannot render herself transparent, invisible. She cannot
frame and present the world to her child without distortion. Her ambivalence means that Pearl never quite knows whether to look at her or
through her. All her messages to Pearl are double messages. When she
instructs, she sows seeds of doubt. When she rebukes, her rebukes are
sharpened by a longing for intimacy, even while she refuses it. When,
before the governor, she defiantly catches Pearl into her protective arms, it
is with the declaration, "She is my happiness!—she is my torture, none the
less! Pearl keeps me here in life! Pearl punishes me too!" Adrienne Rich's
words about the pain of motherhood a century after Hawthorne wrote
those, might have been Hester's:

> My children cause me the most exquisite suffering of which I have
> any experience. It is the suffering of ambivalence: the murderous
> alternation between bitter resentment and raw-edged nerves, and
> blissful gratification and tenderness. Sometimes I seem to myself,

in my feelings toward these tiny guiltless beings, a monster of self-ishness and intolerance . . . And yet at other times I am melted by the sense of their helpless . . . irresistible beauty—their staunch-ness and decency and unselfconsciousness. I love them. But it's in the enormity and inevitability of this love that the sufferings lie.[8]

Love like this is a hard teacher. For Hester, Pearl exists not only to be loved and taught, but to love and teach as well. Hester has much to learn from Pearl. The child's probings expose her blind spots and her self-deceptions. Pearl is not only a symbol, but a questioning, defiant human being, obey-ing her own inner laws, and holding the mirror up to Hester that children hold up to every parent. Pearl's feelings and speech seem "natural" in ways that Hester's are not, having been "denatured" by acculturation. The child embodies a mystery that both awes and baffles Hester. In Pearl she con-fronts the real mystery of procreation that belies the heinousness of her "crime." At moments the parent-child power relationship is overturned, and Hester looks to Pearl for insights that will unlock those mysteries:

> "Art thou my child in very truth?" asked Hester. Nor did she put the question altogether idly, but, for the moment, with a portion of genuine earnestness; for, such was Pearl's wonderful intelligence, that her mother half doubted whether she were not acquainted with the secret spell of her existence, and might not now reveal herself.

Later Hester asks, "half playfully," "Tell me then, what thou art, and who sent thee hither?" But Pearl reverses roles with her: "'Tell me, mother,' said the child, seriously coming up to Hester, and pressing herself close to her knees. 'Do thou tell me!'"

Pearl seeks to strip away the veils of deception that hide her parents from her. She speaks out of intuition, more than she knows, for, as the nar-rator remarks, "Children have always a sympathy in the agitations of those connected with them; always, especially, a sense of any trouble or impend-ing revolution, of whatever kind, in domestic circumstances," and Pearl expresses this "sympathy" with a child's total disregard for tact. As Hester is Pearl's "window," so Pearl is Hester's mirror. In her person, her clothing, and her continual scrutiny, Pearl reflects Hester's scarlet letter back to her, magnified, transformed, beautified, animated, and wholly reinterpreted. She pelts it with wildflowers, copies it upon herself in seaweed, and de-mands that Hester put it back on when once, in the woods, she removes it.

---

8. Rich, *Of Woman Born*, 21.

As she loves her mother, the symbol, too, becomes an object of love. Part of Hester's own transformation surely comes from Pearl's total acceptance of, even insistence on, that most troubling dimension of her identity.

Thus the relationship between mother and daughter becomes a sign of hope on hard and ambiguous terms—hope won at "great price." Other social relations fail Hester, but in their rare moments of intimacy she and Pearl begin to forge a bond that is not only that of mother and child, but of woman and woman. They have, between them, on the edge of society, the beginnings of a sisterhood—a community rooted in shared "womanly strengths." In one of her more moving moments of insight, Hester sees Pearl as a woman:

> Pearl took her mother's hand in both her own, and gazed into her eyes with an earnestness that was seldom seen in her wild and capricious character. The thought occurred to Hester, that the child might really be seeking to approach her with childlike confidence, and doing what she could, and as intelligently as she knew how, to establish a meeting-point of sympathy. It showed Pearl in an unwonted aspect . . . In the little chaos of Pearl's character, there might be seen emerging . . . the steadfast principles of an unflinching courage,—an uncontrollable will—a sturdy pride, which might be disciplined into self-respect,—and a bitter scorn of many things which, when examined, might be found to have the taint of falsehood in them.

With characteristic irony, the narrator makes the point again: perhaps only those who dwell outside the systems of law and regulation that quench the Spirit are in a position to assess the ways they erode their own ends. Together in their "magic circle" Hester and Pearl become a society unto themselves, and as such foreshadow the community gathered around Hester in the years after Arthur's death. At the end of her life, Hester becomes a mother-counselor to women caught in subtler versions of oppression or bewilderment than her own, perhaps, but caught, indeed, and waiting, as she is, for a "new truth" or "coming revelation," brought by a woman into a world that has "grown ripe for it." The vision she imparts is of a larger, fairer, more inclusive society in which women, fully empowered and enfranchised, do not threaten or seduce, but come into full partnership with the men on a basis of mutual respect and shared access to the reins of governance and the authority to interpret the word.

Whether that "word"—inscribed in Scripture, constitutional law, catechism, or simply in the buzz of public discourse—is to be life-giving or death-dealing depends upon those who stand in pulpits or sit at the courtroom bench or speak from podiums or from behind the gates that divide them from the accused and the disenfranchised. At the end of the story we hear what Hester says to her devoted listeners no more clearly than she hears Arthur's election-day sermon, but, like her, we may take or make meaning as we will. Our imaginations will be provoked and our own intentions awakened if we listen for what lies just beneath the words, subtle as breath, powerful as music to touch the heart, sometimes at cross purposes with the mind's logic.

Holding her "Pearl of great price," Hester is compelled to consider what has been bought at such cost, and finally finds the courage to claim it: a hard-won understanding of how far grace extends beyond the law and of a deeper fidelity than she had been taught to imagine or aspire to. At such cost, she has acquired the skill required to navigate the grey area between that grace and the laws of a strict-constructionist theocracy, between nature and culture, between "common sense" and personal intuition, between resistance and accommodation. She has learned to inhabit the middle ground on this "middle earth" where to stand "a little lower than the angels" requires the balance of one who dances on the whitecaps. She has stepped into a freedom so spacious that those to whom it is offered commonly choose captivity instead.

Her legacy to us, and Hawthorne's, is an urgent invitation to consider the nature of true freedom, as Edwards once considered "the nature of true virtue," and to practice it, and to learn in that practice a largeness of heart not often enough exemplified in the institution whose mission is to protect and proclaim the good news of divine love. And to reread the story of that divine love in new, larger, more life-giving terms. And to teach what we find there to our children, and theirs.

Bibliography

Austin, Allen. "Distortion in the (Complete) *Scarlet Letter*." *College English* 23/2 (October 1961).

Buell, Lawrence. *Literary Transcendentalism: Style and Vision in the American Renaissance.* New York: Cornell University Press, 1975.

Donohue, Agnes McNeill. *Hawthorne: Calvin's Ironic Stepchild.* Kent, OH: Kent State University Press, 1985.

Edwards, Jonathan. *Images or Shadows of Divine Things.* Edited by Perry Miller. New Haven: Yale University Press, 1948.

Eliot, T. S. *Four Quartets.* New York: Harcourt, Brace, Jovanovich, 1971.

Feidelson, Charles. *Symbolism and American Literature.* Chicago: University of Chicago Press, 1983.

Franklin, Benjamin. *Autobiography and Other Writings.* Edited by Ormong Seavy. Oxford: Oxford University Press, 1993, 2008.

Friday, Nancy. *My Mother / My Self: The Daughter's Search for Identity.* New York: Delta, 1997.

Goss, E. H. "About Richard Bellingham." *The Magazine of American History with Notes and Queries*, vol. XIII, Mrs. Martha Lamb, editor. NY: Historical Publication Co., Press of Little & Co. Jan-June 1885, p. 266.

Hawthorne, Nathaniel. *The Scarlet Letter.* Original publication, Boston: Ticknor, Reed and Fields, 1850. Now in public domain. All citations in this book are taken from the free online version at http://www.gutenberg.org/ebooks/33.

Jocelin, Elizabeth. *The Mothers Legacie, to Her Unborne Child.* Edited by Robert Lee. Written 1624; published 1853; digitized 2006. Original housed at Oxford University.

Juel, Donald H. *Gospel of Mark.* Interpreting Biblical Texts. Nashville: Abingdon, 1999.

Marsden, George M. *Fundamentalism and American Culture.* Oxford: Oxford University Press, 1980.

Merwin, W. S. *The Rain in the Trees.* New York: Knopf, 1988.

Mohrmann, Margaret E. *Medicine as Ministry.* Cleveland: Pilgrim, 1995.

O'Connor, Flannery. *Mystery and Manners*. New York: Farrar, Straus and Giroux, 1969.

Pope Paul VI. "The Right to Be Born." *The Pope Speaks* 17/4 (1973).

Rich, Adrienne. *Of Woman Born: Motherhood as Experience and Institution*. New York: Norton, 1995.

Sanders, Barry. *A Is for Ox: The Collapse of Literacy and the Rise of Violence in an Electronic Age*. New York: Pantheon, 1994.

Schwartz, Joseph. "Three Aspects of Hawthorne's Puritanism." *New England Quarterly* 36 (1963) 192–208.

Tertullian. *De Cultu Feminarum*.

Thoreau, Henry David. *Walden and Other Writings*. Edited by William Howarth. New York: Modern Library, 1981.

Wills, Garry. *Under God: Religion and American Politics*. New York: Simon & Schuster, 1991.

Ziolkowski, Theodore. *Fictional Transfigurations of Jesus*. Eugene, OR: Wipf & Stock, 2002.